Cast of Characters

The Staff

Norma Gale. An intrepid, if somewhat sarcastic, student nurse doing a three-month stint at an isolation hospital. She's a bit sensitive about her hips.

James Lawrence. A young doctor, he's tall, dark and handsome—and determined to give Norma a hard time. Norma's mother says he's also engaged.

Dr. Morgan Gill. A pompous intern "known on all sides as Morgue."

George Moon. An orderly, he's full of complaints, mostly justified.

Linda Beardsly. A nurse and the Danas' niece, she's smitten with a patient and the main target for Norma's sarcasm, perhaps because she criticized her hips.

Plus other personnel, including **Betty Condit**, a nurse, **Miss Fane**, the night supervisor, and **Dr. Bacon**, the hospital superintendent.

The Patients

Agnes Dana. An elderly German measles patient who clings to her carpetbag and sings "John Brown's Body" at odd times.

William Dana. Agnes' brother, he is a slight, spectacled man with German measles and a black leather thumb guard.

Addison Miller. Ad for short, he's a playboy—a young George Sanders type—currently bedridden with scarlet fever and the object of Linda's desires.

Jason Caddock. A vague, shambling fortyish scarlet fever patient who isn't quite right in the head but appears to be harmless.

Brigg Thomas. Not very talkative, he's a wealthy scarlet fever patient.

Mrs. Evans. A demanding scarlet fever patient

The Police

Inspector Millard Shaw. He's courteous and gentlemanly.

Sergeant Detective Benjamin "Benny" Phipps. He isn't.

The Visitors

Gavin Bart. Linda's cousin and nephew to the Danas, he's tall, dark and handsome, although Dr. Lawrence dimisses him as an "overgrown schoolboy with a pretty face."

Marcilla Thomas. Brigg's wife.

The Unseen

Louise Fish. The fiancee. Although she remains off-stage, she is never far from Norma's thoughts.

Books by Constance & Gwenyth Little

The Grey Mist Murders (1938)*
Black-Headed Pins (1938)*
The Black Gloves (1939)*
Black Corridors (1940)*
The Black Paw (1941)*
The Black Shrouds (1941)
The Black Thumb (1942)*
The Black Rustle (1943)
The Black Honeymoon (1944)*
Great Black Kanba (1944)*
The Black Eye (1945)*
The Black Stocking (1946)*
The Black Goatee (1947)
The Black Coat (1948)*
The Black Piano (1948)
The Black Smith (1950)
The Black House (1950)
The Blackout (1951)
The Black Dream (1952)
The Black Curl (1953)
The Black Iris (1953)

*reprinted by the Rue Morgue Press
as of June 2002

The Black Thumb

by Constance & Gwenyth Little

The Rue Morgue Press
Boulder, Colorado

Printed at Johnson Printing
Boulder, Colorado

The Rue Morgue Press
P.O. Box 4119
Boulder, CO 80306

PRINTED IN THE UNITED STATES OF AMERICA

About the Littles

Although all but one of their books had "black" in the title, the 21 mysteries of Constance (1899-1980) and Gwenyth (1903-1985) Little were far from somber affairs. The two Australian-born sisters from East Orange, New Jersey, were far more interested in coaxing chuckles than in inducing chills from their readers.

Indeed, after their first book, *The Grey Mist Murders*, appeared in 1938, Constance rebuked an interviewer for suggesting that their murders weren't realistic by saying, "Our murderers strangle. We have no sliced-up corpses in our books." However, as the books mounted, the Littles did go in for all sorts of gruesome murder methods—"horrible," was the way their own mother described them—which included the occasional sliced-up corpse.

But the murders were always off stage and tempered by comic scenes in which bodies and other objects, including swimming pools, were constantly disappearing and reappearing. The action took place in large old mansions, boarding houses, hospitals, hotels, or on trains or ocean liners, anywhere the Littles could gather together a large cast of eccentric characters, many of whom seemed to have escaped from a Kaufman play or a Capra movie. The typical Little heroine—each book was a stand-alone—often fell under suspicion herself and turned detective to keep the police from slapping the cuffs on. Whether she was a working woman or a spoiled little rich brat, she always spoke her mind, kept her rather sarcastic sense of humor, and got her man, both murderer and husband. But if marriage was in the offing, it was always on her terms and the vows were taken with more than a touch of cynicism. Love was grand, but it was even grander if the husband could either pitch in with the cooking and cleaning or was wealthy enough to hire household help.

The Littles wrote all their books in bed—"Chairs give one backaches," Gwenyth complained—with Constance providing detailed plot outlines while Gwenyth did the final drafts. Over the years that pattern changed somewhat but Constance always insisted that Gwen "not mess up my clues." Those clues were everywhere, and the Littles made sure there were no loose ends. Seemingly irrelevant events were revealed to be of major significance in the final summation. The plots were often preposterous, a fact often recognized by both the Littles and their characters, all of whom seem to be winking at the reader, almost as if sharing a private joke. You just have to accept the fact that there are different natural laws in that wacky universe created by these sisters.

Like several other Little titles, *The Black Thumb* is set in a private hospital, with many of the large cast of characters being either doctors or nurses. And as a rule, their nurse protagonists were a bit more conscientious about their jobs than most of their other heroines. Even so, the standard of care at this particular hospital makes today's managed health care seem like a desirable option.

The Littles published their two final novels, *The Black Curl* and *The Black Iris*, in 1953, and if they missed writing after that, they were at least able to devote more time to their real passion—traveling. The two made at least three trips around the world at a time when that would have been a major expedition. For more information on the Littles and their books, see the introductions by Tom & Enid Schantz to The Rue Morgue Press editions of *The Black Gloves* and *The Black Honeymoon*.

CHAPTER 1

HEAT PRESSED in through the high screened windows like damp wool and lay against my throat and face with an unpleasant smothering effect. I cursed the choice of a profession that kept me in starched uniforms through the summer and reflected bitterly that the blue-and-white stripes were unbecoming as well as uncomfortable. Authority seemed to go out of its way to chivy the student nurse, and I yearned toward graduation and the time when I need no longer walk around looking like a mattress.

I padded along the corridor, trying to look efficient, and hauled up at the chart desk, where Betty Condit drooped in a state of genteel perspiration.

She said, "Hey! Where are you going?"

I eased myself onto a chair. "Where would I be going—except to disport myself among the exanthemata? I always try to look busy when I'm on duty. I figure it might keep people from asking me to do extra odd jobs."

Betty sniffed, and I glanced at my watch. "What's doing, anyway? Am I going to have trouble with old Jason tonight?"

"Mr. Jason Caddock, scarlet fever," said Betty, yawning, and added without venom, "The old turnip. Sure—he's been quiet all day, so he'll probably want to roam tonight."

"I'll lock his door."

She nodded without interest. "Maybe you better. There's some extra work waiting for you."

I groaned dismally and mopped at my damp neck. "What the devil adults think they're doing with scarlet fever I don't know," I said peevishly. "They ought to leave that sort of thing to children."

"It turned out to be only German measles with these two," she explained. "Their doctor is in with one of them now."

"Nice fellow," I said bitterly. "I'm only a student, but that's what you call a snappy diagnosis, isn't it? When you can't tell a German measle from the local variety?"

I knew that the hospital would not admit German measles if it saw them coming, since the disease was scarcely more troublesome than a cold in the head, but if a patient did come in through a doctor's mistaken diagnosis he had to go through the mill in the usual way and stick around throughout the quarantine period.

So I was loaded with two new patients whom I need never have had.

"They're a brother and sister," Betty explained. "Elderly. And you can't really blame the doctor. He said he thought it was measles, but he wanted to wait another day—only the old dame wouldn't. She raised hell and said measles was very dangerous for people of their age, and she insisted on coming to the hospital at once, where they could have the proper care. You can't tell her, even now, that it's German measles. She declares that she was exposed to what she calls adult scarlet fever, and if it's not measles it's probably scarlet fever."

"I still say the doctor must be a ham."

"What do you know about it?" she demanded with a certain amount of heat, and I realized that the doctor must be young and beautiful.

"Hush!" Betty said suddenly. "Here he comes. Don't look now."

But I felt that it was too hot for finesse, so I turned around and stared—and I could see what she meant right away. I flashed him a brilliant smile, and my only consolation, when he didn't appear to notice it, was that he didn't appear to notice Betty's smile either. His eyes were fixed absently on nothing, but he veered over to the desk and stood before us, pulling abstractedly at his lip. Betty and I slid to our feet and waited expectantly.

He was tall and had very dark hair, and when he finally came to and looked up at us I was vastly surprised to see that his eyes were very blue.

He said thoughtfully, "The trouble with the old bitch—" And then he stopped abruptly and glanced up and down the corridor.

Betty and I quivered, and my face felt like a bowl of jelly, but I managed to keep it in the mold.

"Write that off the record, girls," he said hastily. "What I meant to say is that Mrs. Dana is convinced she has scarlet fever, and she'll be a very sick woman for a few days until she gets bored with the idea. Her brother, Mr. William Dana, won't cause any trouble. He knows he has German measles and he's reading a book and probably won't be ill at all."

Betty said that that was fine, and he cocked an eye at her and went on. "I'll be in and out a good deal—struggling to pull the old lady through."

He went off after that, and Betty and I laughed until I noticed that several lights were glowing along the corridor over the various doors— when I started off on the night's business.

I went to Mrs. Evans' room first because I knew she'd make the loudest racket if left the longest.

She was a woman of about forty-five, with a bad complexion, small eyes, and a large nose. She was officious and talkative and she knew everything. She had been very ill, but she was on the mend, and I think she was rather ashamed of having caught a thing like scarlet fever at her age.

"Girl!" she greeted me. "My bed's uncomfortable, and I'd be appreciative if you'd make it for me."

I knew that she merely wanted to talk about her husband and her three children—she seldom spoke of anything else—but I knew that she would make trouble for me if I didn't do as she asked, so I slipped into the gown that hung by the door and set to work.

She always called me "girl" because she knew that I was only a student doing my three months' stint at the isolation hospital, and she wasn't the sort to hand out a title until it had been earned.

I remade the bed as quickly as possible and answered catch questions at the same time. She finally asked me what I would do if I were married and my husband wanted to play golf every weekend. Would I allow it?

I said, "Yes," but that turned out to be wrong, because a Mrs. Yossel had done just that, and one weekend Mr. Yossel failed to return at all and after a good deal of frantic search was at last found to be living at the club and playing golf every day.

I got away at last and went in to Mr. Thomas, who was a distinct relief. He was a heavy-set man of about forty, still pretty sick, but over the worst of it, and a good patient. Betty had told me that he was quite rich, but he had come to the hospital to avoid infecting his two children who had never had scarlet fever.

He never talked much, so I tried to make a little cheerful conversation for him. I told him about Mrs. Dana, who refused to have German measles and insisted on having something real. He laughed a little and observed, with some feeling, that she did not know when she was well off.

I shifted over to Addison Miller's room with every expectation of enjoying the interlude. Ad Miller was in his thirties—brown hair, brown eyes, and one of the few people I've ever known who looked attractive in bed. He smoked incessantly and was obviously out for a good time whenever he could get it. Linda Beardsly, my relief nurse, had declared herself in love with him but quite honestly admitted that after a lot of spadework she was getting nowhere fast.

Ad Miller greeted me cheerily and then proceeded immediately to lodge a complaint. "Listen, sweetie," he said reasonably, "is there any way—any nice way, of course—to muzzle that brood mare in the next room? She's been singing about John Brown and his blasted body for hours."

"Mrs. Evans?" I said doubtfully. "She never sings. You've been dreaming."

"I have not," he declared emphatically. "I met her in the solarium today—one husband, three children. And she's been singing on and off ever since."

"It's off just now," I said mildly, "but I'll go and tell her you object, if you like."

"Wait a minute," he said cagily. "Has she money or power?"

"Money, no," I replied, "but power by the sackful. She generates her own."

The singing started up just then, and I paused to listen. It was "John Brown's Body," all right—and fairly loud—but after a moment I realized that it was coming from Mrs. Dana's room.

I explained Ad's mistake to him, and he wanted to know all about the new patient.

"I haven't seen her myself," I told him, "but I'm going in there presently, and if she's beautiful I'll come back and tell you. If not I'll merely rap twice on your door, in which case you might as well go to sleep."

I washed my hands for the fifth time in about twenty minutes and wondered idly how long they'd hold out. Ad, watching me, volunteered the information that he did his sleeping in the daytime because the night nurses were prettier. He added that brown eyes, chestnut hair, and a white skin could be quite breathtaking. I glanced into the mirror over the wash basin and identified my ordinary coloring with a quite illogical spasm of annoyance.

Mrs. Dana had finished with John Brown for the time being, and I found her lying back on her pillows, staring at the ceiling. She was gray-haired and elderly and looked thoroughly cross.

"I'm glad to see you're feeling better," I said nursily.

"I'm not better," she replied coldly. "I'm worse; you had better take my temperature."

"A little later," I promised. "Weren't you singing a while ago?"

"I was. And I'll sing if it pleases me."

"Oh, certainly, by all means," I said hastily and tried to slip out, but she called me back peremptorily.

"I want a list of all the patients in this corridor, Nurse."

I hesitated and said uncertainly, "Well, there aren't many."

"Then tell me," she snapped. "And hurry."

"Mr. Thomas, Mrs. Evans, Mr. Miller, Mr. Caddock, your brother, and yourself."

She nodded. "I don't know any of them, but I trust they are all nice people."

"I trust so," I said piously.

"They should be. I hear there is an epidemic of scarlet fever, but my doctor tells me that this floor is composed entirely of private rooms. I understand the riffraff is on the floor below."

"Well—er—" I murmured and left it at that.

"I had to come to the hospital," she went on, "because I haven't had a maid I could trust for years. I know I shall be good for nothing in a few hours, and I've some matters I want to attend to while I'm still capable. Get my suitcase—will you?—and put it by the bed. I think I may be able to attend to my more pressing affairs before I become really ill."

I glanced around the room and saw a large old-fashioned carpetbag reposing in a corner. I hauled it over to the bed and asked rather timidly, "Is this your—er—suitcase?"

"Yes, that's it. It was my grandfather's, you know. He was a traveling salesman just after the Civil War. It's perfectly sound and hardly worn at all, and I can't see paying for a new one while it lasts."

"But you'll probably have to leave it when you go—" I started to warn her.

She cut me short. "No, no, no—nothing of the sort. My doctor promised me—I shall certainly take it home with me when I go. He says something can be done. You fumigate things—or sterilize them—"

"We kipper them," I said and fled.

I made my way to her brother's room to see if there was anything to be done.

But there wasn't, because he wasn't there.

CHAPTER 2

I STOOD in the uncontaminated corridor and frowned at the empty room, and then I remembered Jason Caddock and the fact that I had not yet locked his door. I fled down the hall, hoping against hope, but I was too late. Jason had departed too.

I was exasperated and scared as well. If it were discovered that any of my patients were out taking walks I'd get into trouble, because all germs were supposed to be confined to their own particular rooms.

I knew that Betty had left. It was a few minutes after eight, and she was off at seven. I considered for a moment, chewing nervously at my lip, and then made for the solarium. I thought that I might find them there, and if I could get them back to their rooms and mop up the germs after them, no one need be any the wiser.

As I approached the end of the hall I saw that the solarium was lighted, and I crossed my fingers.

I saw at once that Jason Caddock was not there, but a slight, spectacled, elderly man sat reading in one of the armchairs. He had thin lightish hair and pale eyes, and I noticed that one thumb had a black leather covering.

He lowered the book and blinked at me through the glasses.

"Mr. William Dana?" I asked.

He said, "Yes, Nurse," and got to his feet.

"You're supposed to stay in your room, you know," I said, trying to sound like the night supervisor, whose style I admired. "Will you come back now, please?"

"Yes, Nurse," he repeated and added mildly, "It was kinda hot in that room. I'm not sleepy and I want to read for a while. Be a lot more comfortable in here."

"It's against regulations," I told him. "Come on back to your room now, and I'll see if I can open your transom wider so that you can get more air."

He followed me without protest, and we wended our way to his room, which was directly opposite that of his sister's. The corridor walls of all the rooms were constructed almost entirely of windowpane, and there were shades on the inside, so that the rooms could be made private when it was necessary. I reflected that it would be nice for Mr. Dana and his sister during the day—they could sit up in bed and make faces at each other across the hall.

Mrs. Dana's shade was drawn, but as I opened her brother's door her voice suddenly floated through the transom, dealing with John Brown's body again. William gave a little jump, and his book crashed to the floor. His face puckered like a child about to cry, and he said fretfully, "Make her stop singing that song."

I looked at him in some surprise but said readily enough, "All right, I'll speak to her. But I want to get you into bed first."

He was quite docile, and I made him comfortable and extracted a promise to stay in his room until he was given permission to leave it. I went out and had to clean up his outside door handle, since he had touched it, and then wash my hands again—and all the time I was yearning wistfully back to the kind of hospital where germs and things did not have to be taken so seriously.

I went across to Mrs. Dana, slipped into the interminable apron, and politely requested her to sing no more.

She showed fight at once and said, "Rubbish! I shall sing till dawn if I wish."

"Then I shall have to close your transom," I said firmly. "And I'm afraid your room will be very hot."

"Who's been complaining?" she demanded belligerently.

"Several people. But don't ask me who they are because I wouldn't tell you anyway."

The fight went out of her and a sly expression gleamed from her eyes. "All right, I shall not sing any more. Just leave me, so that I can get on with my affairs. I am holding up as well as I can, but I know it will not be long before I shall have to give myself wholly to my illness."

She had papers spread all over her bed, and the carpetbag seemed to be filled with them too. I wondered how such a mess of stuff could be fumigated, but after all, it was not my worry, so I degermed myself and left her to it.

I began to search through the vacant rooms for Jason Caddock and felt a rising sense of anger at Betty for not having locked him in. We all knew that he wasn't mentally normal, although he was apparently harmless. He was a vague, shambling man in his forties, and he lived with a married sister and washed dishes and helped with the housework. He had caught scarlet fever from some of the nieces and nephews, of which there was a sizable and still-growing number.

I had to go to the phone at last and report Jason missing, and I was given a thorough dressing down that I thought Betty should have shared, although I didn't snitch on her.

I sat down at the desk and tried to relax while the heat poured over and around me. I thought of all the things I might be doing on a hot night that would be vastly more comfortable and entertaining than hanging around a hospital. I began to hope that they would fire me because of Jason and knew all the time that they wouldn't.

I heard the elevator doors open in the outside hall, and two sets of male footsteps presently produced George Moon, an orderly who announced that he was searching for Jason, and Mrs. Dana's doctor.

I rose to my feet, gave George a brief nod, and sent a fancy smile at the doctor. Wrong tactics, probably, because the doctor passed on after according me bare recognition, while George slowed up and finally dropped anchor at the desk.

"What you dames see in them butchers!" he said, looking genuinely puzzled. "They give you the brush-off every time, but you keep on tryin'."

"I haven't an idea in the living world of what you're talking about," I lied haughtily.

"Do you ever smile at me that way?" George went on.

"No,'" I said.

"No," said George. "And why?"

"I shouldn't care to say," I replied distantly. "You might try growing a mustache."

He fingered his upper lip and asked uncertainly, "You ain't kiddin'?"

"When I see it I'll let you know whether I was kidding or not. What about Mr. Caddock?"

"Yeah," said George, "what about him? I guess he'll keep."

But he straightened up and moved off, and shortly afterward Mrs. Dana's doctor came along and made himself comfortable in the chair beside the desk.

"She's gone to sleep," he said, "with stocks and bonds smeared all over her."

"Are they valuable?" I asked sharply. "Because I don't want the responsibility—"

"They are merely a representative collection from the stacks in her safe-deposit vault," he said, pulling out a cigarette case. "She brought them along because she likes to play with them." He lighted the cigarette and rested his head against the wall behind his chair. "I wish to God she'd wake up. I want to talk to her before I go, but I'm afraid to wake her myself. I'd catch hell. Why don't you do it?"

"You want me to get in bad with her? When I have to hang around here all night at the mercy of her room light?"

"Haven't you any finesse?" he asked mildly. "You could take a basin with you and tell her it was time to wash behind her ears, or something. She likes people who do their duty."

"It's no part of my duty to wake a patient unnecessarily," I said, paying him back for ignoring two of my best smiles.

He said, "Tweet, tweet! What makes you nurses so noble and trustworthy?"

I shut my tongue, in behind my teeth until I was able to control it, and then I said almost calmly, "Dr. Bacon and the night supervisor, Miss Fane, are due at any minute for evening rounds. Don't forget, you have your diploma, but I'm still working for mine."

He killed his cigarette and produced a bag of peanuts. "Young woman," he said after he had eaten a couple, "you are, as you point out, but a lowly student—which excuses you to a certain extent. But I feel moved to warn you in regard to your future encounters with less understanding doctors. A nurse simply has not the dast to criticize a doctor to his face. What you say later to your intimate girlfriends is another matter, but what you say to the doctor's face, in the time-honored tradition, is bow; 'Yes, Doctor'; bow; 'No, Doctor'; bow again, and so on."

I said, "Thanks," stiffly, and at that moment Dr. Bacon and Miss Fane pushed through the doors into the wing. Mrs. Dana's doctor stood up immediately, patted my hand, and oozed out.

I caught Miss Fane's eye, and she said in a stern aside, "You will not entertain your friends while you are on duty again."

"But, Miss Fane!" I exclaimed, shocked. "He isn't—he's not my friend. He's Mrs. Dana's—" But she was talking to Dr. Bacon, and they paid no attention to my bleatings.

They did not stay long. Everything was in order, and after they had delivered somewhat of a reprimand about Jason they departed.

Mrs. Dana's doctor appeared again at once and sat down.

"What's your name?" he asked amiably.

"Norma Gale. But listen—you put me in a nasty spot. They thought I was entertaining my boyfriend when you slid off like that."

He laughed, as I knew he was going to. "Oh well, you have no cause to be ashamed. I am wearing both coat and tie, and there are no holes in my socks. Matter of fact, I wanted them to think just that. I was unwilling to meet them in my true colors—Dr. James Lawrence—who mistakes German measles for measles."

"Yes, Doctor," I said and bowed.

"In a sense," he went on, stretching his long legs out comfortably, "you are not so completely innocent as you'd like to make out. You will tell your girlfriends that I sat and chatted with you for a long time—and you will neglect to mention that I was waiting for Mrs. Dana to wake up. Looked at that way, you were entertaining your boyfriend while on duty."

Before I could answer—and I admit that nothing snappy enough had occurred to me—the strains of "John Brown's Body" came floating through Mrs. Dana's transom.

"There she is," I said flatly. "She's awake now."

He stood up. "What do you mean? How do you know?"

"Can't you hear her?" I asked impatiently. "She's been singing that song all night."

He stared at me. "Singing?" he repeated slowly. "But that's impossible. She despises singing, and as far as I know, she's never sung a line in her life."

CHAPTER 3

I LOOKED at him curiously and said after a moment, "You don't know her very well, do you? She's been singing that song all evening."

"I do know her very well," he insisted. "I've known her for about four years. She was my first and, indeed, my only patient for some time. I've pulled her through several serious illnesses, to wit—a cold in the nose, headache, sprained ankle, and cut finger."

He turned away from the desk and headed down the corridor, and I refrained from laughing and trailed after him.

Mrs. Dana had stopped singing when we got to her room. She looked up as the doctor opened the door and greeted him with enthusiasm. "My dear Jim, I'm so glad to see you! I began to think you were never coming. I—er—" She looked beyond him, and her eye fell on me. "Get rid of the nurse," she ordered in a clear, carrying whisper.

I had not actually set foot into her contaminated room, so I made a face at her through the glass, making sure, of course, that she wasn't looking at me, and turned away.

I crossed the corridor and had a look at William Dana. He was sitting up in bed, still reading, and I noticed again the black leather covering on the thumb of his right hand. I had nothing else to do at the moment, so I went in and asked him if he'd like me to look at his thumb and bandage it for him.

It was the only time that William Dana was ever rude to me. His face flushed darkly, and he said venomously, "Get out of here, you silly pest! And don't come back again or I'll—I'll push you out!"

I went at once and mused for a while with bitterness on the gray pall of ingratitude that draped the human scene. I thoughtlessly glanced in at Mrs. Evans as I passed her room, and she immediately made frantic signs to me—as she always did when I was foolish enough to let her catch my eye.

I sighed vastly, went in, and asked her what she wanted.

"It's that abominable singing. I cannot stand it and I will not stand it. Always the same wretched tune."

I clicked my tongue in sympathy. "Don't worry about it any more, Mrs. Evans. I shall have it stopped. How are you feeling tonight?"

"Very poorly," she said promptly. "All the disturbance, you know. And that orderly. What's he looking for, anyway?"

"Oh yes—well—I don't know. Laundry, I believe."

"I believe not," said Mrs. Evans thinly. "I saw him in that room across the hall. Laundry, indeed!"

She referred to a vacant room where George must have turned on the light and given her a perfect view of himself.

"Don't worry about the orderly," I said easily. "He's merely earning his bread and butter. Why don't you try to sleep? It's almost ten o'clock."

"Yes, I think perhaps I should." She settled back onto the pillow. "I must get my health back for the sake of my family. They need me so."

I made her comfortable, and she continued to talk about her family. When I left at last I don't think she noticed it much, which was all right because I figured she was more interested in her conversation than I was.

Mr. Thomas' room was dark, and he appeared to be sleeping, so I did not go in. But I got caught passing Ad Miller's room. Like Mrs. Evans, he made frantic signs to me to come in, so I detoured and asked him what he wanted.

"Company," he said. "Yours."

"Why don't you go to sleep?" I asked. "You know you have to get up early in the morning."

"I can't go to sleep for looking forward to it," he said, eying me like a sheep. "When you slip in here in the early morning and minister to my needs—it points up the whole day."

"You're overdoing it," I said critically.

"Am I? Perhaps, yes. But you don't know how abysmally bored I am."

"I know it's pretty bad," I admitted. "I had scarlet fever once, and it's like being in prison when you're getting well."

"I like you," he said suddenly. "Will you come and see me when I get out of this pesthouse?"

"Do you live in an apartment?"

"Bachelor apartment. Very cozy." He heaved a sigh and added, "I wish to God I were there now."

I gave his bedspread a last twitch and made for the door.

"Will you come and visit me?" he asked insistently.

"Not my type—I'm the selfish kind. I like to be taken out to dinner, dances, and shows."

As I was going out the door he called after me, "That's only a stall, darling. You know you don't get enough time off for dinners, dances, and shows."

I glanced up and down the corridor to see if George was about, but he had disappeared, and I supposed that he had gone down the stairs at the end of the wing and was extending his search to the other floors.

I walked down to the chart desk and hoped that I would be left in peace until Linda Beardsly came to take over.

She appeared ten minutes early and gave me the shock of a lifetime.

"I don't believe it," I said, staring at her.

"Don't be funny. You know why I'm early—I told you. I'm in love."

"You're coming an awful crasher, then," I said, fanning myself with one of the charts. "You can't grab hold of a butterfly. Either you kill it or it gets away, but you can't hold it."

"We'll see," she said lightly. "How do I smell?"

"Perspiration," I said, still fanning. "How would anybody smell in this weather?"

She asked me not to be vulgar and informed me that she never felt the heat.

"Maybe I'd better fall in love, then," I sighed, "if it saves you on a night like this."

Linda straightened her cap and fingered her carefully peroxided curls. "How are my relatives?" she asked idly.

I said, "They're just fine. How are all my folks?"

"I mean my aunt and uncle," she explained impatiently. "They're right here in this wing. Dana."

"The Danas are your relatives?" I asked, surprised.

"Sure are. Mom's family. Pa always said Mom's entire family were crazy—up to and including Mom. But I wouldn't know. I'm not taking sides. Listen, you beat it now and catch some sleep."

I stood up and wriggled myself loose from my clothes, which were sticking to me. "All right, I'm off. Mrs. Dana's doctor is with her, by the way."

"Is he, now?" said Linda, unconsciously elevating her chin. "I was in love with him once. But—well—quite impossible. I realized—"

"Blew a fuse, you mean?"

"Right," said Linda.

I left, then, after warning her to come out of Ad Miller's room at reasonable intervals just in case the other patients wanted some attention.

Unexpectedly she took offense and called after me, "I'm a conscientious nurse, and I *never* neglect my work or let my private life interfere."

I laughed all the way down to the nurses' dining room at Linda calling any part of her life private. Her affairs were always in a show window for anyone to see.

In the dining room Miss Fane hailed me to tell me that Jason had not been found and that they had telephoned to his home, but he had not gone there.

"What was he wearing?" she asked in a worried voice.

"He had only the hospital's pajamas and dressing gown, as usual," I said timidly.

"Yes, but I wondered if he had managed to get some other clothing. I wish you girls would keep him locked in," she said, turning away.

I felt sorry and a bit ashamed about it all, and I made up my mind to hand onto Betty as much as I could remember of the dressing down that had been given to me.

It was too hot to eat much, and I decided to find a comparatively cool spot and try to sleep. I ruled out my own bedroom in the nurses' home as being a hole in the wall and an oven, and in the end I returned to my wing with the intention of trying the solarium.

Linda was not at the desk, and I looked through the windows of the various rooms and eventually discovered her in Mrs. Dana's room. Aunt and niece seemed to be chatting, both mouths going together. However, they appeared to be perfectly amiable, and I figured it as one of those confabs where both parties are talking to themselves but like the sociability of a friendly presence.

The solarium, with windows flung wide on its three sides, was almost comfortably cool. I settled onto a chaise tongue and stayed awake long enough only to wonder if I were breaking a rule.

I slept like the dead, but I was awakened abruptly with a confused sense of having heard a noise and to absolute darkness, when I knew that I had left a floor lamp burning.

There was some sort of movement at the far end of the room, and then the noise started again—several dull thuds, followed by a crash of splintering wood.

I scrambled to my feet in a cold sweat of fear and stood for a moment swaying and trying to clear my head.

It was quiet for a while, and then something stirred and moved, and I could hear footsteps padding away down the corridor. I stumbled blindly through the length of the place and pressed the light switch by the door, and as my eyes focused I saw that one of the chairs had been hacked to pieces.

CHAPTER 4

I STARED at the wreck with a growing feeling of scared amazement. The chair was a basket weave with upholstered cushions, and the cushions had been cut and chopped beyond repair. Both of the frail bamboo arms were smashed in half.

I turned away and crept to the door, but the corridor was blank and empty, and suddenly I was furious with myself. Jason Caddock must be responsible for such a perfectly senseless act of vandalism, and I had let him get away again while I blundered around uselessly in the dark. We all knew that he was a bit queer, and now, apparently, he was loose in the hospital with an ax—or something very like it.

The stairs were next to the solarium, and I ran out and peered down over the banister, but they were empty and quiet. I flew along the corridor to the chart desk, but Linda was not in sight, and I went straight back to Mrs. Dana's room. Linda was there—either still or again—and the two appeared to be chatting. I tapped on the glass and, when Linda glanced up, beckoned frantically.

She came out, and I explained the situation in a hurried undertone. Her forehead wrinkled into a frown, and she kept repeating, "But what do you mean? I don't get it."

"Then get this," I said at last in exasperation. "Stop gaping and talking like a silly parrot and go and lock all the patients' doors—unless you want to find one of them chopped up into several sections."

Her face paled, and she whispered, "My God! I thought you were talking about a chair. What are you saying?"

"Linda," I said furiously, "you lock those doors!"

She moved off, then, but quavered over her shoulder, "Where can I lock me in?"

I ignored her and ran to the telephone. I was still there when she came back up the corridor with the keys in her hand and a whispered assurance that everyone was locked in. She stood close beside me, and I could hear her teeth banging together quite clearly.

I glanced at her over the telephone and muttered, "Stop dramatizing yourself. You could stop those absurd dental gymnastics if you wanted to."

"Certainly I could," she said huffily, "but why should I? I'm scared to death, and it gives me something to do besides having hysterics."

I said, "O God! Keep on clicking, then. Are you sure you locked them all in?"

"Every one," she declared firmly. "I locked old Jason up first of all."

I dropped the phone into its cradle. "Jason!" I squealed. "You mean he's back?"

"Sure he's back. Came in all by himself about half an hour ago. I mean, I didn't see him come in—I noticed his light was on, so I went down to have a look, and there he was in his little bed, sleeping like a baby. I figured he was good to stay put for a few hours after his constitutional, so I didn't bother to lock him in right then. I meant to come back and do it just as soon as I got time, but I've been busy. I fixed him up, of course, and he slept right through everything. But I'd have had to go to the desk for the key and then come back—" She paused, of necessity, to take breath and added brightly, "But I phoned the office and reported him in."

"Did you want me to pat your back?" I asked politely.

She opened her mouth to do battle, but at the same time the elevator door clanged in the hall outside, so she straightened her cap and gave her hair an anticipatory pat instead.

Miss Fane came in, followed by Dr. Morgan Gill, an intern who was known on all sides as Morgue, and George Moon. They acted like a committee and went all the way down the corridor to shake their heads over the broken chair.

Linda was instructed to go into Jason's room and see if there were any sort of weapon concealed there, but she looked carefully at her watch and announced with a good deal of firmness that she was off duty by a margin of a minute and a half. She added unnecessarily that I was now on in her place.

Miss Fane frowned and compressed her lips, and I went into Jason's room without argument, because I knew I'd have to in the end. I did not know whether Miss Fane, Morgue, and George simply wanted to avoid the degerming process that was obligatory when you went in and out of the occupied rooms or whether they were scared, like Linda.

As a matter of fact, Jason was sleeping quite peacefully, and it did not take me three minutes to make sure that there was nothing in the room that could have been used to chop up chairs, so I scrubbed out again and reported to the committee. They looked nonplused and took refuge in some more headshaking. I felt faintly sorry for them because I knew that I should not have known what to do in their place, either.

They became articulate long enough to warn me to keep Jason locked in and then walked slowly along the corridor—Miss Fane and Morgue to the front, George dangling in the rear—and disappeared in the direction of the elevator.

"Well, I'm off," Linda said without waste of time.

"How are your relatives?" I asked and felt a sissy for wanting to keep her with me.

"They're all right," she said impatiently. "Aunt Aggie won't be really ill until the morning—she has too much to do—and Uncle William never gives any trouble. I haven't even said hullo to him—he was sleeping when I came on."

"Why are they both Dana, when she's married?" I asked and knew that I was still craving companionship and didn't really care.

"She married her cousin—same name. He lasted only a few months and retired to the loony bin—poor soul."

She went off in a hurry, then, and I was left alone. I stood by the desk, staring down the corridor nervously considering how to make a getaway if anything savage should appear. A sound behind me brought me whirling around with my heart in my mouth, and I came face to face with George Moon. He had come up in the elevator which had taken Linda down, and I had had no warning of his presence.

He said, "Hello," rather dispiritedly. "I got to search the whole damn lousy floor. The bright idea come to them in the elevator, and they sent me up again."

I had managed to get my breath back and I asked, "Did they tell you what to search for?"

"They'd like an ax," said George disgustedly, "but they'll settle for anything the old drip might-a used to slug that chair."

"You'll probably find something," I said thoughtfully. "He could not have taken it far—whatever it was. He must have gone straight back to bed."

"They always got me huntin' for things around here," George grumbled as he moved off, "and I ain't found nothin' yet. You'd think they'd give up."

I felt vastly more comfortable at having George within call, and as my nervousness subsided I began to feel the heat again. There was not a breath of air stirring, and my hair and clothes stuck to me with damp, smothering persistence. I wondered if I were going to pass out and felt almost cheerful at the prospect. Someone would have to attend to me, then, and I could stretch out and take it easy.

Mrs. Evans' light glowed suddenly in the bulb above her door, and I forgot about passing out and went along to see what she wanted.

She had turned on the light over her bed, and as I unlocked the door and slipped in she said, "Girl, I am simply expiring with the heat! I cannot stand it. And what have you got the door locked for? You'll have to leave that door open."

"Sorry," I said mildly. "I can't leave the door open. It's against—"

"I keep fretting about my husband," she said, serenely unconscious of interrupting. "Nelson is a perfect martyr to the hot weather—he perspires like a fool and he doesn't know what to do for himself when I'm not there. Now I wish you'd go and telephone and find out if he's all right."

Mrs. Evans had been at the hospital long enough for me to know how to handle things of that sort. I wasted no time in argument or in suggestions as to Nelson's mood if he were awakened in the early hours of the morning by someone who merely wanted to know how he felt. I said, "Certainly, Mrs. Evans. Just leave it to me."

"That's right. And you must come and let me know at once."

"I'll come back to your window and raise my right hand if he's all right."

"Yes—well—but I'd sooner you came in and told me. And listen— tell that wretched man next door to go to bed. There's no excuse for anyone to be pacing the floor at this time of night. Simply no sense to it. I believe that's what woke me up—that and the heat."

I wondered whether she was crazy—and if not, what Ad Miller was doing pacing the floor. I soothed her with promises of punishment for anyone who would disturb her rest and departed.

The last time I had noticed Ad he had certainly been in bed and apparently asleep. I saw now that his room was dark, but even as I looked his face seemed to float up against the pane and hang there, suspended.

I caught my breath sharply, and at the same time he grinned and beckoned, and the rest of his body came into focus, correctly attached to his neck.

I sighed and entered, and he switched on his light.

"What are you doing out of bed?" I asked crossly.

He gave me a charming smile. "I'm convalescent, and I feel great. I can't possibly sleep at night—I never do, you know. Always do my sleeping in the daytime."

"Yes, of course," I murmured coldly. "You spend the night hot-spotting around."

He seated himself on the edge of the bed and asked mildly, "Did I sound too boastful? But I must do something to amuse myself in this plague spot—and boasting is one of the most fascinating sports known to the human race."

"For some people, I suppose."

"For all people—and you included, sweetie. Everybody boasts, but vastly different methods are used by different people. Take the well-to-do suburban housewife—in her set boasting is right out beyond the pale—mustn't do it—not a word of boast—but walk into her cleanly house and the place reeks of it. There might be a spinning wheel to prove and proclaim decent New England Mayflower ancestry. And then there's Grandfather's portrait hung prominently—not to display his unfortunate features—but to show that Grandfather had enough money to have his portrait painted and to scotch all rumors that he might have been a bum."

"I'm sorry to make hash of your little theories," I said, "but my grandfather was a bum—he stole horses for a living—and yet he made time to have his portrait painted, and Mother has it hanging on the wall. Now do get into bed and at least pretend you're asleep, whether you are or not."

He sighed resignedly, but allowed himself to be settled, and I urged him to behave himself as I went out the door.

I saw George disappearing into the solarium, apparently still searching, and then I remembered that the rooms were still locked and I went quietly along and unlocked them. I made sure that Jason was still locked in, but I felt that the others would be all right as long as he could not get out.

I went on down to the solarium after that and stood at the door, watching George work. I even gave him a few words of advice, which he assured me, with some heat, were unnecessary.

I presently turned to glance automatically at the signal lights over the doors and saw Mrs. Dana standing in the middle of the corridor in her nightgown.

CHAPTER 5

I LEFT George in mid-search and went flying down the corridor, and to Mrs. Dana I gave all I had of stern, outraged nurse. "You are not supposed to leave your room under any circumstances without express permission," I said, enjoying myself. "It is one of our strictest rules. The corridors are uncontaminated—"

"Teach your granny!" she said shortly, but she allowed herself to be led back to her room.

"Did you touch anything?" I asked, getting her into bed. "Outside your room, I mean."

"I touched nothing. I thought I heard something out there, that's all. I shan't go out again—didn't know your rules were so strict."

Her face was rather gray, and I saw that her hands were shaking. I asked uneasily, "What was it? Did something frighten you?"

"Nothing of the sort," she said irritably. "Is there anything so unusual about my hearing a noise outside? The way you people parade around all night out there—it's scandalous."

"I'm afraid I'll have to lock your door," I said doubtfully. "I can't have you running around."

"You'll do nothing of the kind!" she yelled. "I won't have it. I've told you I didn't understand the rules and I've promised to stay here. Now let's have no more about it."

"All right," I said hastily. "Now try and get some sleep, will you?"

"I'd like nothing better." She dropped her head onto the pillow and closed her eyes. "Just take yourself off and leave me alone."

I turned off her light and scrubbed out, and then I stood in the corridor for a while, wondering whether I ought to lock her in, anyway. But she'd be sure to hear it and raise the roof, and in the end I decided, with some misgiving, to let it go.

I went quietly down to the solarium again and gave George a bit of a start, since he was draped comfortably on the chaise longue, smoking a cigarette.

"You shouldn't take your job so seriously," I said. "It'll tell on your health someday."

"Oh, nuts!" said George.

"Do you want to get fired?"

"You said it."

"Why, for, heaven's sake?"

"Being an orderly," said George with simplicity, "is one hell of a lousy life."

"Then why on earth don't you resign and avoid the stigma of being fired?"

"You could-a left out the fancy words and said that in half the time," said George, exhibiting a little sarcasm. "You dames don't understand these things. If I'm fired that's one thing, but if I leave I'm throwin' up a job, and I couldn't look myself in the face."

"Oh," I said vaguely, "I guess I have an undeveloped sense of honor. But suppose you get on with your search."

He heaved himself off the chaise longue and disposed of his cigarette. "Yeah, sure. And if I get my damn head hacked off while I'm doin' it I don't guess you'd care."

"Not much," I said blithely.

"I gotta do them rooms with the patients in."

"All right, I'll introduce you. Let's go."

We went to Mr. Thomas' room first, and he woke up and asked if it were morning.

I said no, but George had lost a valuable stickpin and he was very anxious to find it, if Mr. Thomas did not mind. Mr. Thomas said he supposed it was all right, but for God's sake to hurry up.

George hurried up and drew a blank, and as we were scrubbing out Mr. Thomas suggested, with a certain amount of sarcasm, that we drop in again sometime.

We went in to Mr. Dana's room next, but he gave us no trouble. He opened his eyes and watched us incuriously, and in the hope that he would think it was hospital routine for his room to be searched in the early hours of the morning, I made no explanation and merely asked him how he felt.

He said, "Just dandy, thank you, Nurse," and apparently dropped off to sleep again.

"I'm glad you didn't pull that stickpin gag in there," George said when we got out. "I'm tellin' you now, I don't like it."

"Why?"

"I don't want them guys thinkin' I'd go around wearin' a stickpin."

"You're too sensitive," I said, "but I'll think up something else. Come on."

"I got my pride," said George as we walked into Mrs. Dana's room.

Apparently Mrs. Dana had been just drowsing off to sleep, and she woke up with a start.

"What on earth do you want now? What is it?" she demanded shrilly.

I had to think quickly, and I didn't do so well. "George lost his collar button on the floor somewhere today, Mrs. Dana, and if you don't mind he'd like to search your room."

George, searching in silence, flushed a bright crimson, and Mrs. Dana glared. I held her eye firmly, but with humility; and after a moment she narrowed her lips and eyes and said briefly, "Hand me my purse."

I handed it over, and she burrowed for a moment and hauled out a quarter. "Give him this and tell him to buy a new collar button and get out of my room—both of you."

"Well, I—I couldn't," I said uncomfortably. "In the first place, that quarter is now contaminated, and anyway, the—the collar button has a sentimental value. George's first wife gave it to him—"

"How many times has he been married?" she interrupted, and I could see the light of gossip in her eye.

"Three times," I replied, with no thought but to hold her interest until George finished his job. I knew he was a bachelor, and proud of it, but I figured that it didn't matter.

But it must have annoyed him, because at that moment he either threw or dropped the ancient carpetbag onto the floor with a crash. Mrs. Dana and I jumped and turned our heads to see him milling savagely through the papers with which the thing was crammed.

Mrs. Dana started to yell at him to get himself out of her bag and her room or she'd set the police on him, and we finished and departed hurriedly around a fusillade of threats and curses.

George stopped dead when we got into the corridor and said stubbornly, "You gotta think up something else to tell them—and I wanta hear it first."

"Think up something yourself," I said in exasperation. "It's your search. I'll go and take a rest."

He backed down at once. "Now wait a minute. What are you sore about? I can't go in and start lookin' around. You're the nurse, you got to talk to them."

We argued it back and forth for some time and then we made for Ad Miller's room with a story all prepared. Ad had his light on and was reading, but he put the book aside and welcomed us courteously. "Hello, everybody. Come in and take a seat."

George started searching without a word, and I asked Ad how he felt.

"Darling, I've told you so many times. I am bored. "

"I'm sorry," I murmured, with one eye on George. "Is there anything I can do?"

"You can stay in here and amuse me and let the other patients languish."

"I'd get fired."

Ad said, "I'll give you a job," in a rather abstracted manner and peered down at George, who was on his hands and knees, looking under the bed. "Is it an institutional secret," he added, "or may I ask what the orderly is doing?"

"We're sorry to disturb you," I said glibly, "but one of the doctors lost an important formula on this floor, and George has been ordered to search the entire wing."

"In the small hours of the morning?" Ad murmured, looking me squarely in the eye. "Waking the patients?"

I looked back at him helplessly and found nothing to say.

"You won't take it amiss if I say I don't believe you?"

I straightened my apron, which was already straight, and said feebly, "Oh well—orders, you know."

Ad looked at George again and asked pleasantly, "Did you find it, fella?"

"No sir," said George, preparing to depart. "Not here, I guess."

"Wait a minute—you haven't searched me or the bed."

George glanced at the bed, which was bare of covering and very obviously contained only Ad Miller in a pair of thin pajamas, his book, and two pillows.

"Couldn't possibly be there, sir," said George.

Ad smiled. "Something big, then. The good doctor must have written his formula on a scroll of parchment."

"We'd better go, George," I said hastily.

"Before he spills the beans," Ad agreed.

We got out in a hurry, and while we were washing our hands in the corridor George observed, "That's a no-good story too—he caught on. We got to think up another one."

"I can't—my brains are dead. And anyway, if he didn't believe our story he still doesn't know what we're looking for."

"Him and us both."

"Don't be silly. We know it must be something like an ax. Come on, now, we've only one more to do—Mrs. Evans. I searched Jason's room myself."

I turned on Mrs. Evans' light and gave George a push to start him off. She woke up at once, but she didn't wait for an explanation at all. She declared that she had only just dropped off after one of her worst bouts of insomnia, and she stated positively that she was going to sue the hospital, naming me as a representative or an accessory, and claiming damages for a shattered nervous system.

George had finished his search and was out of the room before she was half through, and I merely waited until she was obliged to stave off strangling by taking a breath, when I said loudly, "It's a matter of saving a life."

She stopped in midsentence and stared. "What's that?"

"It's the only thing that can save this particular patient," I said, blushing to hear myself talking such rubbish, "and it must be found."

She ate it up and became quite concerned. She wanted all the details, and when I finally managed to get away she made me promise to let her know the instant the formula was found.

George was waiting for me at the chart desk.

"Boy, oh, boy! Did you get it!"

I said, "Pooh! She was eating out of my hand."

He went off to report the failure of his search, and I sat down and thought it over. It seemed to me that Jason would not have had time to hide his ax, or whatever it was, anywhere but on this floor. I had been almost on his heels out of the solarium, and immediately afterward he had been in bed.

I began to wonder whether a lunatic from another floor had wandered up, and then I shivered and tried to think of something else.

I pulled myself together and started to work on my report, and at the same time Mrs. Dana began to sing "John Brown's Body."

CHAPTER 6

I DREW a sharp, exasperated breath and made my way down to Mrs. Dana's room. It was in darkness, but I went in and switched on the light.

"What's the matter, Mrs. Dana?" I asked, preparing to do battle.

She turned her head on the pillow and frowned at me. "What do you mean?" she asked crossly. "Nothing's the matter."

"Will you please stop singing, then? The other patients are complaining, and I can hear you all the way up at the desk."

She made no reply for a moment, and then said sullenly, "I was not singing."

"All right," I said cheerfully. "Try and go to sleep, will you?"

"I can try," she said acidly, "but it isn't very easy with you running in here every few minutes."

I promised to leave her in peace and returned to the desk. Everything was quiet, and I noticed that the heat was less oppressive, although there was not enough change to bring hope for a cooler day.

I was busy enough, but the hours dragged, and when Betty Condit appeared at seven o'clock I felt as though I had been on duty for a week.

Betty gave me a bright good morning and then asked what was the matter and added that I looked as though I had seen a ghost.

"If it had been only a matter of a ghost I'd be feeling fine," I said gloomily. I told her of the night's events, and in the cheerful light of morning she was inclined to call us a bunch of sissies. I shrugged and went on down to fortify myself with food and hot coffee.

I slept heavily through the heat of the morning and dreamed that Jason was chopping up furniture with an ax and singing "John Brown's Body" at the same time.

I woke up in the afternoon feeling rested and relaxed and I made up my mind to forget hospital business altogether. I hauled out two of my dresses and spent a lot of time redecorating them, and then I discovered that they had looked better the way they were. In the end I was almost ten minutes late getting to my post.

Betty had a battered look about her, and I asked warily, "Trouble?"

She rolled her eyes. "That Dana woman! No nausea, and you couldn't ask for a better temperature and pulse. But she's been cutting up like a fiend—groaning and carrying on. Even when the visitors were here."

I said, "O God! Visiting day! I'd forgotten."

Visitors were permitted for two hours in the afternoon twice a week, and one hour in the evening once a week, and were generally regarded as a curse and a black cross—except by the patients.

Betty yawned a couple of times and took her departure, and I went on down to see Mrs. Dana, who was groaning loudly.

I skipped into her room with nursy cheerfulness dripping out of my ears. "Well, well, I hear you've had a bad day," I trilled obnoxiously.

"You must be glad that you're so nearly over it."

She stopped groaning and gave me a chilly, suspicious stare. "What do you mean, nearly over it? Scarlet fever lasts for days."

"Ooh yes, of course, but evidently you haven't heard of the latest methods of treatment. The way they do it now, you are ill for only one day—and after that it's merely a matter of convalescence, and you feel marvelous."

To my utter astonishment the suspicion died out of her face and she nodded. "Well, that's what my doctor told me, but I thought he was merely trying to cheer me up and I didn't believe him."

It was a particularly fortunate coincidence, I thought, trying to keep my face straight, that I had potted onto the same silly lie as Dr. Lawrence. Mrs. Dana let out a few more groans, but I didn't worry about it, since I figured that she was simply trying to get in as many as possible before the time was up.

Visitors were due from eight to nine, and at seven forty-five by the clock Mrs. Dana recovered and began to pretty up. She said that her nephew might drop in.

"Would that be Linda's brother?" I asked chattily.

"No," she snapped. "Of my two brothers-in-law, one was trash—and that was Linda's father."

Just before eight o'clock I moved all the beds up to the windows that gave on the corridor, locked all the doors, and stood by.

Mrs. Thomas was the first to arrive, and I watched her go down the corridor with her heels clacking, dressed in correct summer sportswear which did not suit her in the slightest. She and Mr. Thomas never had any trouble conversing through the glass, since they both had carrying voices. In fact, when they got going the rest of the bunch had no chance at all. I listened for a while, and it went something like this:

"How are you, Brigg?"

"All right, Marcella. How are you?"

"Fine."

"And the children?"

"Just grand."

"That's good. Are you feeling the heat too much?"

"Oh no. Out at the house it's cool at night."

"That's good."

I closed my ears and took a look at the other visitors who had drifted in.

There were two nondescript women in front of Mrs. Evans' door, and beside them, peering in at Ad Miller, were two women and a man. The women were flashy and ornamented with jewels, which tantalized me, because I could not make up my mind as to whether they were real or not. I tore my eyes away at last, because one of the women caught me looking at her.

There was no one for Mrs. Dana or for William Dana, but Jason Caddock had his sister and sister's girlfriend. The sister was trying to deliver a small parcel through the transom, so I hurried down to take it and explain that I would give it to him later. I was too late, as it happened, for Jason had it when I got there and was already unwrapping it. He promptly stuck his tongue out at me and, having found that the parcel contained a wedge of pie, he ate it in three bites.

I pursed my lips in disapproval, as I had seen it done by the graduates, and left the scene of the crime. As I walked slowly along the corridor I felt, as always on visitors' night, like a policeman on the beat.

Mrs. Thomas was leaving, I noticed, and shortly after she had gone an unknown tall, dark, and handsome appeared. He obviously did not know his way around and was peering uncertainly into various rooms, so I decided to give him a hand.

"Can I help you?" I asked prettily.

He turned around and took me in at a glance—mattress-striped dress, voluminous apron, cotton stockings, and shoes whose only excuse was their comfort.

"You're not Linda," he said and smiled nicely.

"Are you looking for her?" I asked and wondered what possessed Linda to fool around with a dilettante like Ad Miller when this knew her.

He said, "No, as a matter of fact, we're not speaking at the moment. We had a quarrel."

"I'm sorry," I murmured and reflected that Linda should have her head examined.

"Not at all—we prefer it that way. Can't stand each other at any price, you see, and we've always been thrown together; so if we're not speaking it makes it easier to avoid each other."

I put two and two together at that point and said, "I guess you must be Linda's cousin."

"Right. And I'm here to do my duty by Aunt Aggie and Uncle William."

"Your father was the one who was not trash," I said, thinking out loud.

He laughed with apparent genuine enjoyment, but I felt myself blushing hotly.

"I'll show you where their rooms are," I said hastily, but he caught at my arm.

"I'm not in any hurry. Can't we talk for a while? I'd like you to have a better opinion of me than the one you must have formed on Linda's say-so."

"She has hardly mentioned you," I assured him. "Only once or twice—and all she called you was 'that rat.' "

"She can do much better than that. Perhaps she thinks better of me than I had supposed."

We were called to order by a persistent, sharp tapping, which turned out to be Mrs. Dana, who could just see us by pressing her face against the glass.

He murmured, "Duty calls, I see," gave me a little bow, and made his way leisurely to his aunt's room, where he leaned gracefully against the door and lighted a cigarette. Mrs. Dana started pouring words out in a steady stream, and I wondered if he could hear any of them. At any rate, he nodded wisely at regular intervals.

I reminded myself that it was rude to stare and tore my eyes away.

Mr. Thomas had two men at his door, and their voices were almost as loud as Mrs. Thomas'. The conversation now went something like this:

"Joe was on the green in one and took a par three, while Harry was in the trap, so he sinks the approach, and Joe was fit to be tied."

"But who won the match?" from Mr. Thomas.

"Then Harry gets behind a tree on the sixteenth, and he whacks the tree and goes back behind it." Loud guffaws here.

"Yes," from Mr. Thomas. "But who won the match? "

I wanted to know, myself, by that time, but I didn't feel that dignity would allow me to linger further, so I moved off. On my way to the desk I noticed that Mrs. Evans' two girlfriends were having a heated argument, while Mrs. Evans had her ear glued to the window.

Visitors were supposed to be all out by nine o'clock, and at ten minutes to nine there was no one left except Linda's cousin, who had moved over to William Dana's door and was doing a little talking himself.

"You'll be all right, Uncle," he was saying. "Don't worry—just take it easy, be calm, relax—you'll be all right."

I decided that he was a bit mixed up and had meant that speech for his aunt. As far as I could see, William Dana never bothered about anything—much less his health.

At two minutes to nine the cousin bade adieu to his relatives, passed me by with a bright smile and a wink, and took himself off to the elevator.

I walked down the corridor and unlocked the doors, and I had got all the way back to the desk when I realized that I had thoughtlessly unlocked Jason's door as well.

I dropped my keys, had to scramble frantically on the floor for them, and turned around just in time to see Jason disappearing into the stairwell at the far end of the corridor.

CHAPTER SEVEN

I MADE time and a half down that corridor and ran down two flights of stairs, but there was no sign of Jason, and everything was quiet. I listened for a while and then slowly climbed the stairs again, cursing Jason and myself and wondering how on earth he had disappeared so quickly. But it was a large hospital, I reflected, and there were any amount of places where he might have hidden himself. He knew enough to realize that the hunt would be up as soon as his room was found to be empty, and he had a sly talent for avoiding people.

I went back to the desk, picked up the phone, and grimly told on myself. The receiver gave forth blasting noises, but I don't exactly know what was said to me because I held it away from my ear and didn't listen.

When the phone had ceased to crackle I put it down, and since William Dana's light was glowing in the wall above his door I went along to see what he wanted.

"I have nothing to read," he said, blinking amiably through his glasses.

I said, "Well," and wondered what he expected me to do about it.

He made it clearer. "I should like you to get me a book."

"I don't know where I could get one," I said, shaking my head.

"Go to my sister's room—she brought several with her."

I promised to do what I could and went out, wondering crossly how I was to get my work done if I was to take on the duties of a blasted librarian as well.

Mrs. Dana was going through the interminable papers in her carpetbag and gave me only a brief, impatient glance. "Thank you, Nurse, but I shan't need you around any more. I feel completely recovered."

"Nice going," I said dryly. "I hope you enjoyed your illness."

She jerked her head up and her eyes narrowed, so I hastily changed the subject. "Your brother wants one of your books."

"Oh." She glanced at the bedside table. "Take one of those—I've finished them. But tell William he's to go to sleep early. Don't forget, now—I mean it. Tell him to put his light out early and sleep quietly until morning."

I took one of the books across to William and briefly delivered his sister's message.

To my surprise he reared up and showed some spirit. "You go back and tell her I'll do what I like."

"All right," I said admiringly, "I'll tell her where to head in—from you."

"No—no, you needn't do that. Just tell her I'll go to sleep when I please."

"Yes, I see. And then shall I come back and tell you what she said?"

He said, "Yes," so innocently, that I dropped the sarcasm then and there.

I noticed his thumb again and asked, "Hadn't I better change that bandage for you?"

I watched his face darken to an angry red, and his mouth opened and closed twice before any words came. When he spoke the voice was almost guttural, but the only word I could distinguish was "out," so I left with no further argument. I wondered why he was so acutely sensitive about the thumb and I decided to put it all on his chart for the doctors to figure out.

I had to go to Mr. Thomas' room after that and was told that he wanted his window opened in a certain way which he declared would make for better circulation of the air in his room. He said he always had his windows at home opened that way in the hot weather and that it kept his house quite cool.

I tried to comply, and as I fussed with the sash I asked cheerfully, "How are you doing?"

"Very well, indeed. I was allowed out into the solarium this afternoon."

"That was nice."

"That's what you think," said Mr. Thomas, with a reminiscent chuckle. "What a gang!"

"Why? Who was there?" I asked curiously.

"That Mrs. Evans, for one. Somebody should have muzzled her years ago. And the Miller fellow—he smoked cigarettes the whole time we were there and kept saying, 'You are wrong, my dear lady.' Which kept the Evans woman going nicely, because she hates to be contradicted.

"There was also a peculiar item by the name of Caddock who boasted that he had hoodwinked the entire hospital and gone out for a walk last night."

I pricked up my ears at that and wondered who had been responsible for allowing Jason the run of the solarium.

"Did he explain how he had managed it?" I asked, trying to sound casual.

"He was pretty vague about that part of it," Mr. Thomas admitted. "Something about dodging all the nurses and slipping out the front door."

"Oh, nonsense!" I said firmly. "The front door! Right through the lobby and past the office in his pajamas?"

Mr. Thomas gave me a look from under a cocked eyebrow. "Maybe you were looking for Caddock last night when the orderly searched my room?"

For a blank moment I could not remember which of the stories we had told Mr. Thomas, and while my mind was still darting frantically he laughed. "Don't worry," he said. "I didn't really mind. But just the same, I don't believe George ever wore a stickpin in his life."

I got out my professional manner and wrapped it around my confusion. "Too much imagination, Mr. Thomas. Mr. Caddock did skip out of the wing for a few hours, but he was finally located with no harm having been done."

Mr. Thomas said, "Hmm," and I scrubbed out in a hurry before he could think up any more embarrassing questions.

I ran right into George Moon, who didn't have sense enough to get out of my way.

"There you go," I said crossly, "and I haven't washed my hands outside yet. If you get scarlet fever maybe it will teach you not to bump into people."

"Listen," said George. "I had the scarlet fever before you was born, and if I thought I had a chance to get it again I'd stand on my head tryin'. Maybe you think I wouldn't like to put my feet up for a while and have one of you dames bringin' me breakfast in bed."

"If you came up here to look for Jason," I said coldly, "you'd better get on with it."

He nodded gloomily. "Ever since the old lunatic came in here I been spendin' my life lookin' for him. I ain't found him yet and I hope I never do."

"I think that's mutiny," I said, examining my overwashed hands with some concern.

"What?"

"Oh, go on about your work. And don't start up here, either, because Jason went down the stairs, and I'm quite sure that he did not come back:"

George lounged off and disappeared into the stairwell, and I went on with my work. I was very busy, and when Mrs. Dana started to sing "John Brown's Body," just before Linda was due, I had no time to go in and put a stop to it. Her voice was not particularly loud, but it had a curiously penetrating quality which was very irritating.

She was still at it when Linda came on, and I said peevishly, "Listen to that, will you! You said she never sang, and that goes on all the time. I can't do a thing with her—and the other patients all kicking."

"I never said she didn't sing," Linda replied easily. "Seems to me I've heard her working on that ditty before—I think it was one evening when I went to visit her, and she was sitting on the porch. I never heard her sing at any other time, though, come to think of it."

"Well, she's yours now," I said, relaxing in anticipation of food and coffee. "God keep you both. If the superintendent or the governor of the board wishes to confer with me I may be reached in the dining room."

Linda gave my figure a frank, appraising stare. "Don't eat too much—I've noticed that your hips are filling out a little lately."

I placed that as a deliberate lie to get my goat and I spoke hotly. "Look to your own figure, girl. You've had two outstandingly handsome males—your aunt's nephew and your aunt's doctor—practically served up to you on a plate, and you muffed them both. It seems to me that you'd do better to forget hips that don't belong to you and—"

"All right, all right," said Linda. "I was thinking of something else when they taught us what to do for hemorrhage, so for God's sake don't have one. I certainly can't imagine anyone in her right mind wanting that ratty cousin of mine, but I'll admit I mismanaged *l'affaire* Lawrence."

"You mismanaged what?" I asked, calming down.

"You heard me."

"Listen, friend," I said, recovering my temper completely. "I was excited, but I apologize. Only you mustn't ever mention hips to me. They've caused me hours of agonizing anxiety, as you should see my Aunt Hattie's, and I'm supposed to favor her."

"Not at all," said Linda magnificently. "I shall not even think of your hips again—much less mention them."

I said, "Thank you," and bowed. She bowed in return, and I departed to the outside corridor, where I ran straight into Dr. Lawrence.

He was smoothing his hair in front of a small mirror, and when he saw me he said, "I guess I am."

"Am what?" I asked.

"Handsome. I heard you say so, and I thought I'd look and see."

I felt myself blushing furiously and I asked feebly, "How—how much of that conversation did you hear?"

"Most of it, I think—very entertaining. But about that nephew of Mrs. Dana's—I think you have a somewhat exaggerated idea. He's nothing, really—overgrown schoolboy with a pretty face."

The elevator doors opened, and I slid silently within and hid myself in the darkest corner.

I mentally damned my hips and ate an enormous meal, and then I went straight to my bedroom, despite the heat, because I could not have faced the solarium again.

I had forgotten to tell Linda that Jason was missing and I was so uneasy about the omission that I returned to my post ten minutes ahead of time. Linda, however, was quite indifferent.

"I don't give a damn if he never comes back. One less to take care of."

The business of the chopped chair still gave me nervous chills whenever I thought about it, and I wondered a little at her unconcern.

"How long did you spend with Ad Miller?" I asked after a moment.

She said airily, "No longer than necessary," but there was a guilty gleam in her eye.

"I'd like to know how long necessary was," I said grimly, but she was already on her way to the elevator.

I set about my duties listlessly, under the oppressive weight of the heat, and I was uncomfortably conscious of a growing sense of uneasiness. The wing was deathly quiet, and I could not rid my mind of a recurring picture of Jason on the prowl with a hatchet.

I had been at the desk for a while, working on charts and my report, and when I caught myself looking over my shoulder for the fourth time, I gave up and started slowly down the corridor. As I came abreast of Mrs. Dana's room I stopped and stared in surprise and annoyance. Her door was wide open.

"She must have done that herself," I thought, frowning, "trying to get more air."

The room was dark, and there was no sound from the bed. I thought she might be awake, since she was neither snoring nor breathing heavily, but she said nothing and made no movement when I closed the door.

I walked on slowly for a few steps, and then suddenly I turned around and went back to Mrs. Dana's room.

I switched on the light this time and turned to look at the bed.

Mrs. Dana had been chopped and mutilated almost beyond recognition.

CHAPTER 8

DURING the night there was only one graduate nurse on duty for each three floors, and that meant that I was in sole charge of the wing. I think it was that more than anything that kept me from screaming or fainting. I remember switching the light off and stumbling out of the room, and then I leaned up against the wall in the corridor for a while until my legs stopped buckling under me and my breathing became more normal.

The quiet, dimly lighted wing seemed steeped in horror and eerily menaced by a prowling Jason with his bloody hatchet, and I was to blame because I had unlocked his door.

But habit is strong, and I had months of training behind me, and after a few moments I was walking almost steadily to the desk. I gasped my story into the phone and then just sat there, with goose-pimples pricking my skin on one of the hottest nights I have ever known.

I heard the elevator at last, and Morgue Gill came striding into the wing, followed by George Moon. With the two of them towering comfortingly over me, a slight reaction set in, and I began to tremble. I had difficulty with my tongue and teeth, but after a bit of gibbering I managed to indicate Mrs. Dana's room. Morgue became very much the fine, brave young doctor and told me, with a touch of severity, that I was not much of a nurse if I allowed anything that might happen in a hospital to upset me.

Anger steadied me again, and I opened my mouth to tell him that this was not anything, but no voice came out, and anyway, Morgue and George had already started down the corridor. They went into Mrs. Dana's room and switched on the light—and when they came out again, a good deal more quickly than they had gone in, I drew quite a deep breath and felt distinctly better.

I saw Morgue say something to George, and then he went back into the room again while George came along to the desk and picked up the telephone.

I turned away and did not listen, and after a while Morgue appeared and signaled for me. When I joined him I saw that he had features, and particularly eyebrows, arranged to express grave concern and also rocklike dependability. I had seen it done in the movies, myself.

"This is a terrible thing," he said, and the severe touch was still there. "It was that man Caddock undoubtedly. I cannot understand why he is allowed to roam the building every night. I'm afraid it's going to be bad for you, Miss Gale. Carelessness about locking his door."

I was feeling almost steady by that time, and I said hotly, "Mr. Caddock's illness is diagnosed as scarlet fever, not homicidal mania, and I treat him as a scarlet-fever patient. Diagnosis is the responsibility of the doctors and has nothing to do with me. The hospital is not equipped to handle mental patients, as you doctors very well know."

Morgue's handsome eyebrows drooped a little, and I saw the transition to the young intern sticking doggedly to the right diagnosis in the faces of the superintendent and the entire staff. "There was no indication of any real abnormality," he said, and I knew he was rehearsing rather than talking to me. "Quite harmless—stake my reputation—"

I couldn't be bothered any further about setting the blame, and I said tiredly, "She's dead?"

He nodded, said, "Murdered," and moved off to the telephone where I heard him summoning Linda to the floor.

We waited for a while after that in dreary silence. Linda was the first to appear, and she came around the corner from the elevator with her eyes popping. She was given the facts, and I advised her to stay away from Mrs. Dana's room, but of course she must needs go straight down and have a look.

She came back with her face green and told me, in a sick whisper, that she'd never be the same again.

I said, "Oh, buck up, you'll see worse than that before you're through training."

"I hope I'll never see my aunt lying murdered again," she said and, dropping her head on the desk, began to cry.

I had forgotten the relationship and I felt conscience-stricken. "I'm sorry, Linda," I said rather helplessly. "It must be terrible for you. I didn't remember that she was your aunt."

We sat there for a while until the elevator unloaded a group of people. I saw Miss Fane and Dr. Bacon and a couple of nurses, and there were some strange men. Linda and I stood up, and I tried to make myself as small as possible, but Miss Fane's eyes found mine, and her expression boded ill for me. I think she would have spoken to me then and there but for Dr. Bacon, who said, "It's down here," and diverted her toward Mrs. Dana's room, where Morgue and George were mounting guard.

Linda mopped at her wet eyes with a ball of damp handkerchief. "What shall I do about Uncle William? I'll never be able to tell him. I can't—he won't know what to do without her."

"Don't worry about it now," I said nervously. "What are they all doing down there, anyway?"

Linda looked down the corridor and said, "It's the police. I know one of those fellows—Benny Phipps. He has a girlfriend here—one of the girls in the west wing—only they quarreled. She said he was some sort of a policeman. She had him to dinner, and this aunt of hers was there— Aunt Viola—and Benny refused to wear a tie. She was mad as the devil because Aunt Viola is quite ritzy. So they had a fight."

I clicked my tongue in sympathy, and then we noticed that Ad Miller's light was on. Linda jumped up, but I pushed her back. "Miss Fane is around, and I'm supposed to be on duty here."

She said, "All right," rather listlessly, and I went on down the corridor.

Miss Fane was standing outside Mrs. Dana's door, and she said sharply, "What is it?"

I indicated the light, and she nodded and moved closer to me. "If the patients are curious tell them that Mrs. Dana has developed complications and is being moved to another wing."

I said, "Yes, Miss Fane," and turned toward Ad Miller's room. It was in darkness, but Ad's face, round and white, was flattened eerily against the window.

I opened the door and said, "Get into bed, please, Mr. Miller."

"Not me," he replied firmly. "I'm here for the duration of the excitement. Something is going on, and I don't intend to miss it. You can satisfy your conscience by writing 'insubordination' on my chart."

"What do you want, then? Your light's on."

"I want you to supply the subtitles. I can see, but I cannot hear."

"It's nothing that would interest you," I said formally. "Mrs. Dana has developed complications and is being moved to another wing."

He turned a cool eye on me and observed, "Yet it does interest me. I have a pressing desire to know why Inspector Shaw is summoned to view Mrs. Dana's complications and to superintend her removal to another wing."

I had a moment of irritation, when I reflected that in one way or another policemen certainly got around. They seemed to be recognized far and wide.

To Ad I said flatly, "Odd, isn't it?"

"Too odd. They should have the mayor as well. Mrs. Dana is not going to like being fobbed off with a mere inspector when she has an important thing like complications."

I shrugged and turned away. "If you won't go back to bed will you at least try and keep out of sight?"

He moved around in front of me and said, "Wait a minute. You'll have to give me a better story than that one."

"I've had my instructions," I said coldly, "and you've had the only story you're going to get. Now let me out of here because I'm busy."

He put on a faint, charming smile and stepped aside. "You are quite right, of course, and I know when I'm licked. Is friend Linda on the floor? I thought I saw her."

"She is, but you might as well forget about her. She's busy too."

I went out, and while I was washing my hands in the corridor they took Mrs. Dana away. She was entirely covered by a blanket, even to her face and head, and I was conscious all the time of Ad Miller staring through his window.

I dried my hands and turned around and saw that William Dana had come out of his room. He was standing in the corridor, staring after the retreating stretcher with its gruesome burden.

I hurried to his side, and he turned a white terrified face to me.

"What are they doing to Aggie?" he whispered. "Have they found out?"

CHAPTER 9

THE GROUP moving along with the stretcher had disappeared around the corner in the direction of the elevator, and I urged William back into his room in a hurry, for fear someone would come back and see him.

"Please get back into bed. You know that the patients are not supposed to leave their rooms."

He seemed a bit dazed and he obeyed without protest, but his frightened eyes never left my face. I felt that he had a right to know about his sister and that someone should tell him, and I said, "I'll send Linda to you. She'll explain."

He nodded and whispered, "Hurry, please."

I went back to the desk, where Linda was just returning the telephone to its cradle. "O God!" she wailed. "He doesn't answer."

"Who?"

"Gavin—my cousin. I must get hold of him—he's the only other relative."

"Give him time," I said reasonably. "He's out for the evening, I suppose, but he'll get back eventually. You can try him again later. Right now you'd better go along and break it to your uncle; he's waiting for you."

She collapsed onto a chair and moaned, "I can't—that's one thing I can't do."

"But, Linda," I protested, "you'll have to. It wouldn't be right for me to do it; he'd much prefer to hear it from you."

"He'd much prefer not to hear it at all. But since he has to, it doesn't matter who tells him." She started to mop at her eyes again, and I knew that I was lost. "Oh, Norma, please—"

I went grimly down to William's room and found him standing at the window. "You should be in bed," I said briskly. "You must remember that you're ill."

"I'm not ill," he said petulantly. "It's silly being in a hospital when you're not ill."

I forbore to mention the rules and red tape with which he was wrapped up since he had been admitted, and plunged nervously into the business at hand.

"I am afraid your sister—"

"Where's Linda?" he asked abruptly. "Why doesn't she come?"

I had an impression that he was afraid to hear what I had to tell him, but I plodded on.

"Linda is very much upset, and she asked me to tell you. Your—your sister is dead."

At once I had a sense of having put it too bluntly, and I watched him anxiously.

"Dead?" he said vaguely. "But— Dead? What was it? You didn't expect it, did you? I mean, she was all right when she came in here. Quite healthy. Nothing but that little rash. I had it too." He jerked his head around and fastened his troubled eyes on my face. "What do you mean, Nurse? She can't be dead."

"If you'll only go back to bed I'll tell you what I can."

He went at once, and when I had settled him I gave him a brief outline of what had happened. I said that someone had come in and given her several blows and that she had died under them. I said nothing of the horrid mutilation of her face and body, but my own memory of the thing must have shown in my face, for he said suddenly, "Was it bad? Dreadful? Who did it to her?"

He seemed quite calm and almost as though he did not care at all, and I was puzzled and uneasy.

"What did they hit her with?" he asked.

I said quite truthfully that I did not know and refrained from adding that I could guess well enough.

He dropped his head back onto the pillow, while his hands moved restlessly. After a moment he began to pray, and tears slid from the corners of his eyes.

I heaved a sigh of relief, went quietly out of the room and back to the desk.

Linda had been telephoning again, but she looked up and asked fearfully, "How was it?"

"It's all right—he's crying a little now. But I think you ought to go down; he asked for you."

"Oh." She stood up, looking relieved. "I'm glad it's all right. Of course I'll go."

She went off, and I sat at the desk and watched the dimly lighted corridor. I tried to keep my mind a blank, but the image of a demented Jason dragging a hatchet became so insistent that I stood up and backed against the wall to make sure that he could not creep up behind me.

I was still standing like that when I saw Linda leave her uncle's room. She did not turn up the corridor, as I had expected, but went quietly across to Mrs. Dana's room instead. I knew that she herself had locked the door on instructions from one of the policemen, and while I watched her she deliberately unlocked it again and slipped inside.

I knew that she was doing wrong and might get into trouble and I started hastily after her. As I passed I saw that Ad Miller was still standing at his window, looking out. In the room next to his Mrs. Evans was also out of bed, with her nose flattened against the pane, and across the hall Mr. Thomas stood peering out with his eyebrows slightly raised. I reflected that you could not keep the fear and unrest out of the rooms—it seeped in, despite all your efforts. It was a good deal easier, I thought, to keep their scarlet-fever bugs shut in with them.

As I approached Mrs. Dana's room Linda slipped out, and I saw that she was clutching the old carpetbag.

"Linda, you'll be fired for this," I whispered, horrified. "What do you think you're doing?"

"I don't care," she said defiantly. "Uncle William says he must have it, and it's the only way to keep him quiet. What's the difference, anyway? They were both German measles, and as for the papers, they're nothing but duplicates. All her stuff is in the bank—these were just playthings. After all, no one saw me, and you needn't tell."

"Of course I won't tell," I said, "but, for God's sake, hurry. I don't suppose we'll be left alone here for long."

Nor were we. Linda had barely disappeared into her uncle's room when George Moon hove into sight, conducting two men to the desk. He signaled to me in a rather lordly manner, and I hurried to join them. George introduced the two men with a flourish and the use of their full names—Inspector Millard Shaw, previously recognized by Ad Miller, and Sergeant Detective Benjamin Phipps, rumored as a martyr to his conviction that the dinner tie was superfluous. He was wearing a tie now, I noticed, and I decided after a second glance at it that he might just as well have gone bareneck.

The inspector, courteous and gentlemanly, wanted to ask me a few questions and suggested that I sit down. Benny Phipps retired to the background and amused himself with a toothpick.

I was taken through the events of the evening to the last detail, and I made a conscientious effort to remember everything. Linda returned halfway through the proceedings and waited quietly until the inspector had finished with me.

He turned to her afterward and said, "I understand you are on duty while Miss Gale goes to supper."

Linda said, "Yes," and at his request went on to give an account of the time during my absence.

The patients had been restless, she said, and she had supposed it was the heat. "Mrs. Evans called me first and wanted her bed remade. She's always up to that trick—I guess it's the only thing she can think of to get us in there so that she can talk. Then Mr. Thomas wanted his window and transom jiggled around to match each other so he'd get more air. Mrs. Dana wanted"—there was the suggestion of a pause here before Linda went on smoothly—"she was my aunt, you know, and she wanted to talk for a little while."

I decided privately that what Mrs. Dana had wanted was her carpetbag and that Linda had very nearly tripped herself into saying so.

Mr. Miller had called her once and insisted on talking, but she had left him as soon as she could manage to break away. And Linda made it sound as though she really had made the break at the first possible opportunity.

Her uncle William had called her next and had asked her to phone his nephew to bring him a collection of books.

"Did you do it?" Inspector Shaw asked.

"Well, no—not yet. I couldn't very well phone Gavin in the middle of the night and, anyway, I was too busy. Mrs. Evans and Mr. Thomas both called me in again. They both—and particularly Mrs. Evans—claimed that they could not stand the heat, and they wanted me to tell the hospital authorities that something would have to be done about it. So then I came back to the desk and sat down, and Norma came on."

The inspector sat digesting it all for a while, and then he nodded and stood up. Benny Phipps moved in from the shadows and put his toothpick to rest, and the two of them went on down to Mrs. Dana's room.

They came back after what I think was a brief search, and the inspector said, "I'm leaving Phipps here. We haven't picked up Jason Caddock yet, and I don't want you to be alone. But we expect to have him soon, and there's nothing for you to worry about."

He went off, and Linda and I turned to gaze at Benny, who removed the toothpick and seemed about to speak.

And at that moment a high, masculine voice somewhere down the corridor began to sing "John Brown's Body."

CHAPTER 10

THE HAIR moved along my scalp, and I found myself staring foolishly at Benny's toothpick, which had fallen to the floor.

The singing stopped rather abruptly, and Benny spoke.

"Who in hell's that?"

"I think—it sounds like my uncle," Linda quavered.

I stopped swallowing air and pulled myself together. "I'd better go down and see if he's all right," I said firmly.

Linda said she'd come with me, and Benny just came along without saying anything.

William's room was lighted, and he was sitting on the edge of the bed, apparently studying the floor. Linda and I went in after a preliminary scuffle with Benny, who tried to tag along. We convinced him, after a certain amount of argument, that it was necessary for him to stay outside and watch the proceedings through the window.

William looked up as Linda and I came in and put on our gowns. "What's the matter?" he asked.

"Were you singing just now, Uncle William?"

He said, "Yes," and his eyes slipped from Linda to me and back again.

"Well, you're giving us the creeps singing that song like Aunt Aggie was always doing," Linda said querulously.

William returned his gaze to the floor. "I can't sleep—it's too hot."

"But why do you have to sing that song?" Linda persisted.

"It's the only song I can remember," William said, suddenly irritable. "I've nothing interesting to read and nothing to do, and I'll sing if I like."

"Not too loudly, then," Linda cautioned, "or I'll have to close your transom so you won't disturb the other patients."

"You never closed Aggie's transom," he said resentfully. "She was singing all the time—I heard her. She was allowed to disturb me."

Linda registered shocked reproof. "Why, how can you talk that way, Uncle William? And poor Aunt Aggie only just—"

"Dead," William supplied. He lowered his head, and to my distress he began to weep audibly.

Linda soothed him, and I turned away and left the room after the usual disrobing and hand washing. Out in the corridor, in accordance with rules, I washed my hands again, and Benny lounged over to watch the procedure with lofty disapproval. "Nonsense. In the first place, you can't wash germs off, I know. You gotta boil them. And in the second place, you already washed your hands before you come out."

"In the first place," I explained, "we are not supposed to boil our hands because we might want to use them again, and in the second place, I had to touch the inside of the door in order to let myself out—so I have to wash again."

"Rules and regulations!" Benny hissed, tossing his toothpick around excitedly. "Modern civilization! We lived through that there now Stone Age without none of this truck—and lived better. The simple life—"

"How was the Stone Age?" I asked courteously. "I, personally, never lived at that time."

"Don't be ridickerlous," Benny growled, and at the same moment the phone rang, and I had to race for it.

I was informed that Jason Caddock had been found out in the grounds, fast asleep, and that Sergeant Detective Phipps was wanted down in the main lobby.

I replaced the phone with relief flooding over me like a cool shower and gave Benny his message. He nodded and said he was glad to go. "I don't know how you dames stand it—hangin' around this germ bin all night. So long, girlie."

He departed, and Linda came out of William's room and made her way to the desk via the wash basin.

"How is your uncle now?" I asked.

She said that he was lying down and seemed all right but that he was not sleeping, and she intended to ask Miss Anderson, the graduate nurse for our floor and two floors below us, if he might have a sedative. "Uncle William never sleeps well, anyway," she explained, "and what with having poor Aunt Aggie on his mind, he'll never get off unless he takes something. Where's that Phipps?"

I told her about Jason having been found, and she gave a hefty sigh of relief. "Isn't it awful? For him to have done a thing like that? And then— well, I mean— Well, I guess I'll go along, then. Bye-bye."

I knew what she had left hanging in the air, of course. If I had kept Jason's door locked Mrs. Dana would still be living and that I was, there-fore, actually responsible for her death. I was suddenly so acutely miser-able that I laid my head on the desk and shed a few tears.

I was interrupted by a tap on the shoulder, and I swung around in terror, but it was only the Danas' Dr. Lawrence.

I mopped hastily at my wet face, and he asked, "What's the matter? Frightened?"

"No," I said shakily. "Remorseful."

He sat down, and I thought he was looking rather sober, for him. "Why remorseful?"

I explained briefly, and he said, "Forget it. Someone should have found out that the man was dangerous."

"That's what I told Morgue," I said, beginning to feel a bit better, "when he blamed me. But just the same, you can't get around the fact that—"

"That one of you young nurses would have been done in if you'd kept the door locked. At least Mrs. Dana was older and had lived a lot of her life—so what's the odds? I can't understand, though, why they didn't know he was loco. Dr. Bacon is no fool. Of course Morgue is an ass of the first water. He was two classes below me at school, and he was famous then."

"Famous for what?" I asked.

"For being the most outstanding dope since 1878."

I couldn't help laughing, but I said, "I think he's doing all right here."

"Oh well," Dr. Lawrence said, getting up, "he's the studious type, and that always helps. I thought I'd look in on poor William—I suppose he's awake."

I nodded. "I guess he is. He doesn't sleep much."

He went off and was back again in a few minutes. "He's awake, but he obviously doesn't want to talk, so I offered my sympathy and left."

He sat down by the desk again, but he did not say anything, so I started to work on the charts.

He was silent for a few minutes, and then he stirred and said thoughtfully, "They picked up Caddock, all right, but they couldn't find his bloody weapon, although they looked high and low. They settled on a small hatchet in the gardener's shed finally. The thing was in its usual place, according to the gardener, and was quite free from any stains, but Jason is supposed to have taken it, used it, cleaned it, and returned it—even if he is nuts. All very possible, mark you, but if I were you I'd keep a wary eye open just in case there's something wrong with the figuring."

I caught my breath sharply and abandoned the charts, but before I could say anything he stood up.

"Well, good night," he said lightly. "I can't think why I make myself so familiar with a mere student—and one who doesn't even stand up when I approach any more. But I was ever a democratic soul."

He took himself off, and I was left with a now active and growing fear. What had he meant, anyhow? Suppose the police were wrong about the gardener's hatchet and the real weapon had not been found—what did it matter, so long as they had Jason safely locked away? And yet although I had tried to keep my mind away from it I knew what James Lawrence had meant when he told me to keep my eyes open. There was a terrifying possibility that Jason had had nothing to do with Mrs. Dana's murder.

I stood up abruptly and marched myself into the small diet kitchen, where I set about making coffee and buttered toast to bolster my morale. Yet all the time I was working I had one eye on the door to make certain that nothing followed me in, which resulted in my burning the toast and spilling the coffee all over the floor. The cleaning up took some time, and when I got back to the desk I was wondering whether I could possibly get the charts done before time for the morning baths.

Before sitting down I glanced along the corridor, and the glance became a wide stare.

At the far end of the hall the light was on in the solarium.

CHAPTER 11

I REALIZED after a few moments that my teeth were banging together, and I remembered what I had told Linda, so I straightened my cap
and apron and closed my mouth firmly. I wanted to believe that the solarium lights had been on all night, but I knew that I would have noticed
them, and I forced myself to face the probability that they had been
switched on while I was in the kitchen having my coffee. I felt fairly
certain that no one had passed the kitchen while I was there, and I decided, at last, that someone must have come up the stairs at the far end of
the corridor. Perhaps Miss Anderson.

I stopped theorizing and began to walk slowly down the hall. I looked
into the occupied rooms as I went and assured myself that they were all
dark and that everyone was in bed.

I approached the solarium on wobbly legs, but to my vast relief the
place was empty. I looked around curiously and saw that two chairs had
been drawn up to one of the opened windows, as though two people had
sat there together, looking out over the well-lighted driveway and the
grounds below.

I switched the lights off and turned away. The solarium was always
cleaned out after the patients had been there, and the two chairs would not
have been left in that position. And yet, I thought, irritated at my own
uneasiness, there was probably some perfectly simple explanation.

Miss Anderson was at the desk when I got back. She smiled at me
and said, "Hello. I have a sedative for Mr. Dana. I intended to get here
before this, but we had some trouble downstairs—little girl crying for her
mother."

"He might be asleep," I said. "He's quiet, anyway."

"I'll go along and have a look at him."

I returned to my neglected charts and worked feverishly until Miss
Anderson came back. She said that William had been awake, so she had
given him his sedative, and he should have a nice sleep. I glanced at the
clock and saw that it was something after four—which meant that I'd
have to wake William out of his nice sleep in a couple of hours and clean
him up, according to rules.

However, I let it go and merely asked Miss Anderson if she had put
the light on in the solarium.

She looked vaguely down the corridor and said, "No, of course not. It's out, isn't it?"

"It was on," I explained. "Somebody put it on while I was having my coffee."

She shook her head without much interest and said, "I'm sure I don't know who could have done it, but I'll ask around."

"Let me know if you find out, then. I hate the idea that it went on by itself."

She laughed. "Oh, don't be nervous. They found Mr. Caddock and took him off, so I'm sure everything will be all right now."

I said, "I guess so," rather doubtfully and wished that I could feel as sure about it as she did.

She went off, and I worked hard until six o'clock, when I started the morning wash-ups.

I began with Mr. Thomas, as usual, because he was the most good-natured.

"You're a little late this morning," he observed.

"A little," I admitted.

"Have a nap?" he asked amiably.

"Heavens, no! I've been very busy."

"Oh yes," he said, looking at me with more attention. "There was some trouble during the night. I heard the commotion in the hall. What happened?"

"Oh, Mrs. Dana went bad on us and had to be moved," I said carelessly.

"What was the matter with her?"

"Complications of some sort."

"Well, that's too bad," said Mr. Thomas. He pulled an expression of proper concern over his face for a moment and then wiped it off and said heartily, "I'm really on the road to recovery now. I'll be out of here soon— and glad to be back in harness, I can tell you."

I left him to his happy anticipations and went in to Ad Miller.

Ad was sound asleep, and I had to wake him. He opened his eyes reluctantly and gave me a look of pained reproach. "I don't know how much longer I can take this," he said, yawning elegantly. "Awakened every morning at the time when I do my best sleeping—and for nothing."

"Take a look at the dawn," I suggested. "A lot of people swear by it."

He glanced at the window, frowned, and closed his eyes for a moment. "I have heard people speak well of it," he admitted sleepily. "But there are those who like long tramps in the country and even stewed prunes, I believe. Tastes differ, you know."

"You seem a bit confused this morning," I said cheerfully.

"And why not? I have had fearful nightmares—not to mention all the excitement of Mrs. Dana's exit."

I washed his face in silence, and when he was able to speak again he asked curiously, "What actually killed her?"

I looked up quickly. "What do you mean?"

"Oh, what do I mean! Come on out from behind all that innocence. I saw them take her away, and her head was completely covered—which means, in any language, that she was dead. Furthermore, the local constabulary sent a couple of bloodhounds, which rules out scarlet fever, or even complications. And I want to know what it's all about."

"I'm sorry," I said firmly, "but I can't say."

"You mean you won't."

I was scrubbing out by that time, and I said with finality, "I mean that I can't afford to get fired just to satisfy your curiosity."

I went on to William Dana's room, feeling doubtful and reluctant. Routine was important, and I was supposed to follow it, and yet I knew that William needed his sleep. However, I stuck to routine and roused him, feeling mean and guilty all the while.

He woke up with a start and blinked at me nervously.

"I'm sorry," I said gently. "I'll finish as quickly as I can, and then you can go back to sleep."

He nodded, and I set to work, and by the time I had finished he was already asleep again. I glanced at his bandaged thumb and decided to tell Miss Anderson about it, since I did not dare to mention it to him again.

Mrs. Evans was the last, and I found her already awake. I supposed that this was her usual rising hour, anyway, because a woman who took such exquisite care of husband, children, and house would have to start pretty early in the morning.

She prattled along in the usual fashion until she came to junior, when a new fact emerged. Junior's two upper front teeth were false—he had lost the original brace in a football game. I was mildly surprised, because I could have sworn I'd known all there was to know about the Evans family.

She suddenly left the domestic scene in midair and spoke angrily. "Listen, it's bad enough having that man Miller on one side of me, staying awake until all hours and walking around his room, but when you put another on the other side who does nothing but pace up and down the

floor until six o'clock in the morning it is simply going too far, and something will have to be done."

I was washing my hands at the basin, and I kept my face averted
while my mind pictured the room to which she referred.

It was vacant and had been vacant for some time.

CHAPTER 12

I DRIED my hands slowly and said as casually as I could, "Surely it
couldn't have been as bad as that."

"But it was!" she squeaked. "He wasn't making so much noise—just
walking up and down, up and down. As a matter of fact, I could just
barely hear him, but the monotony, you know, gave me the creeps. I don't
like it, and you'll have to tell him to stay in his bed. He's new, isn't he?"

"How do you know he isn't a woman?" I asked, stalling for time.

"A woman?" She seemed surprised. "It sounded like a man to me.
Heavy tread, but walking quietly. Do you see what I mean? I kept waiting
for the footsteps, and then every once in a while they'd stop. It nearly
drove me crazy. Was it a woman?"

"Well—no. I'll see what I can do about it," I said and tried to get out
of the room.

"Wait, wait!" she shrilled. "I almost forgot—goodness! What was
wrong with Mrs. Dana last night?" I sighed and offered the usual complications, and to my relief she accepted it without any trouble. She clicked
her tongue and said that it was too bad and how was she this morning?

I said, "Pretty bad," and accompanied it by a quite involuntary shud-
der.

Betty was already on when I got back to the desk, and she was fairly
quivering with excitement.

"Isn't it awful? What happened, anyway?"

"Where did you hear about it?" I asked.

"Oh, it's all over the hospital— all the girls are talking."

I felt suddenly dreadfully tired. I did not want to talk about Mrs. Dana
or anything else and I decided to skip breakfast and go straight to bed. I
felt that if I went to the nurses' dining room I'd have to spend my time
answering questions instead of eating, anyway.

After Betty and I had disposed of our business I finished up by telling
her that everything was in order with two minor exceptions. "Two people

are in the habit of coming up to this floor and meeting in the solarium, and there is a ghost man in 42, which is otherwise vacant, as you know."

She gave a faint scream and gasped, "What do you mean? You're kidding, aren't you? I'm terrified of ghosts."

On my way to the nurses' building I met Miss Fane, and I conscientiously told her of the solarium lights and the two chairs—and also of Mrs. Evans' tale of a man pacing in the vacant room next to her.

But Miss Fane, standing in bright sunlight under a blue sky, smiled at me and shook her head a little. "You girls must realize that the patients are always imagining things. You shouldn't take it too seriously. As for the solarium, the police probably left the light on there, and the chairs were in that position during the afternoon. The maids don't always arrange the chairs—or even clean properly—as I have every reason to know."

She dismissed me without any reference to my fault in having unlocked Jason's door, and I went to bed feeling a good deal easier in my mind. I slept heavily at first and then I began to have nightmares and eventually woke up screaming. It was not quite two o'clock, but I was hungry and decided to dress and have something to eat and perhaps have a nap later on.

I went out into hot, bright sunlight and walked slowly through the beautifully kept grounds. I admired a posy here and there and had stopped to sniff at a bright red one, when a tall figure rose up off the grass and bowed to me.

It was Dr. Lawrence, and he said cheerfully, "Good morning. You're up early. I had not expected you for quite some time."

"Were you waiting for me?" I asked curiously.

"Yes, certainly. I've been waiting since one o'clock."

"But aren't you busy?" I asked in some surprise. "I mean, your patients— And how do you get away with lying on the grass?"

"The sign refers to dogs only," he said, "and it's cooler down there than in the sun. As to my six patients, only one of them is ill, and that is William Dana."

"I never saw anyone lying on hospital grass before," I declared. "I'm sure it's illegal in some way."

"Quite permissible, on the contrary," he assured me. "Admittedly, Morgue dropped around a short while ago with a stretcher and a couple of orderlies and wanted to grab me off to add to his collection of patients, but I slapped him down."

"Morgue is conscientious and takes his job seriously," I said, "and I feel sure he'd know the difference between you and a patient. So I don't believe your story."

We had reached the hospital, and I tried to head for the nurses' dining room, but Dr. Lawrence steered me firmly around to the coffee shop. "The last time I tried to eat in that nurses' hash room," he said mildly, "they were rude to me. In fact, to make a long story short, they refused to serve me."

We sat down at one of the minute tables in the coffee shop and ordered the various bits and pieces of delicate nourishment that are offered by the ladies who run hospital coffee shops. Dr. Lawrence drew a pencil line across the painted top of the table and told me I was to keep my food on my own side.

I poured cream into my coffee and settled back comfortably. "You said you were waiting for me out there on the grass. Does that mean you want to be my fella, or something?"

He glanced up at me with a faint smile and elevated one eyebrow. "I must make a point of speaking to Miss Fane about you students. She ought to plane some of the corners off you—you're too crude. However, to give a frank answer to a frank question, I have some interest in being your fella, and probably shall accept your invitation to that effect."

"My what?" I said feebly.

"You and that Condit threw beaming smiles at me when I first came here, and I chose you—that's all. No offense to that Condit, of course."

"Her name is Betty, not 'that,' " I said, recovering myself, "and I'm quite sure she doesn't want you, in any case."

"What has happened to womankind, anyway?" Dr. Lawrence said plaintively. "You attempt honorably to boost the Condit to me instead of giving her a few sly digs. And I suppose the next time you see her you'll talk about the weather instead of sneering at her for having failed where you succeeded."

I carefully removed my sandwich from its waxed-paper wrapping and then said helplessly, "I'm afraid I got lost several hundred words ago. What are we talking about—if you know, yourself? Isn't it possible for us to have a decent, sensible conversation?"

"Oh well, if you prefer the Morgue type—" He pulled his face into lines of deep gloom and began to speak in a low, serious voice. "The case interested me to such a degree that I felt obliged to go back and study it further. The hair was blond, and the incidental coloring—no doubt affected by a morbid growth of cosmetic—"

I nudged him violently at that point, because Morgue had appeared at the door.

Dr. Lawrence glanced over his shoulder, and Morgue made his way to our table and asked if he might join us.

Dr. Lawrence said, "Certainly, if you bring your own table or eat on your lap."

Morgue laughed politely but without mirth and sat down, and a spoon went clattering to the floor. He stooped to pick it up, but Dr. Lawrence stopped him.

"Leave it," he said firmly, "or allow the lady to get it. I was at school with you, Morgan Gill, and I know that if you attempt to retrieve that spoon you will undoubtedly bring a cup and saucer down on your head."

Morgue gave Dr. Lawrence a forgiving little smile, and I said, "If you mean me, I'm not going to pick it up. I think Dr. Gill ought to practice until he can do it properly, regardless of the disasters in between."

Morgue gave me a look of cold reproof and turned his attention to Dr. Lawrence. He tried to launch out into a case of some sort, but he was stopped before he had properly started.

"Not now, fella," Dr. Lawrence said. "I'm very busy now. As soon as I finish here I have to go out on the lawn again."

Morgue drew back, looking thoroughly offended, and picked up the menu.

Dr. Lawrence gave him a friendly tap on the arm and said, "Try the egg sandwich—it's not bad, really—and besides, it's all they have left."

Morgue turned to the gentlewoman who awaited his order and said, "Oh well, then, I guess I'll have an egg sandwich."

The gentlewoman withdrew; I poured more coffee; Morgue stared with a puzzled frown at the pencil line running through the middle of the table, and Dr. Lawrence was silent for a full minute.

He spoke suddenly at the end of the minute. "Know something, Norma? I found out about that 'John Brown's Body' thing. Seems Mrs. Dana used to sing it on her front porch on the first day of every month throughout the year—and at no other time."

CHAPTER 13

I SAT silent for a while picturing Mrs. Dana singing that absurd song on her front porch on the first of each month, and then I said uneasily,

"She must have been a bit cracked—don't you think so?"

Morgue cleared his throat, lowered his eyebrows, and delivered an opinion.

"There was no indication of a feeble mind, imbecility, or insanity. She had a very normal mentality."

"That's what you said about Jason Caddock," I said, still uneasy, "only you used fewer words."

"Exactly," said Morgue, swelling with sudden triumph. "Exactly, my dear girl. And I have been confirmed in my opinion. I heard about it this morning."

"You mean they've decided that Jason is sane?" I asked anxiously.

Morgue nodded. "They found no sign of cerebral excitement."

Dr. Lawrence, frowning and absently tapping on the table with a fork, said suddenly, "The case is not closed, then."

Morgue had eaten his sandwich in exactly three and a half bites, and he proceeded to drink an entire cup of coffee in one gulp. When the rush of waters had subsided he said, "No. Naturally the police are not quite satisfied."

"I don't see how they can be sure about Jason," I wailed. "You know he was a bit silly."

"Caddock is definitely moronic," said Morgue, enjoying himself more every minute, "but not in any sense insanic."

Unfortunately for Morgue, he was called away at that point, and he was not the sort to ignore the voice of duty. He went promptly, with only one wistful backward glance.

I turned to Dr. Lawrence and said earnestly, "Listen—be frank and come clean. Could there possibly be such a word as 'insanic'?"

"I have never heard of it," said Dr. Lawrence tolerantly, "but if Morgue wants to use it I don't see who can stop him. He gets carried away by his own eloquence sometimes."

"Well, there isn't any doubt about what he means, though. And if Jason is not insanic, then somebody up there is. I can't think of any reasonable impulse that would lead you to chop up chairs."

"Can't you?" He dropped the fork he had been handling and looked at me—not really seeing me, but with his thoughts turned inward. After a moment he said slowly, "It could have been practice—a tryout. You'd want to be sure—you'd *have* to be sure—that your weapon was adequate."

I shivered and whispered, "Please! This—this gets worse as it goes along. The police are not satisfied with Jason, and I'm not either, as a matter of fact. There's something queer— I'm going to ask for company;

I don't see why I should stay on the floor alone."

"I agree with that," said Dr. Lawrence, nodding. "That's why I'm going home to sleep now, so that I'll be fresh to stay up with you all night. I'll need to be fresh—or you'll get fresh first."

"What are you talking about?" I asked as he paused to take in breath.

"Nothing—nothing at all. Finish playing around with that bit of egg on your plate, will you? I have to go, and you've overstayed your date already."

I rose to my feet with a good deal of dignity and said, "I'm sorry, you should have nudged me."

We went out onto the grounds, and Dr. Lawrence said, "Good-by for the present, then, until tonight," and made for his car. I walked on slowly through the early-afternoon heat toward the nurses' home. I had a lecture at five, and I thought that I'd better try to get some more sleep before then.

I slept, all right, but the nightmares started again, and after the second one I gave up and read a book instead. That was much better, since it kept my mind more or less occupied with the foolish doings of the characters.

At five o'clock I went to the lecture, and that was all right, too, almost interesting in spots.

When I went on duty at seven I was feeling pretty well. I was about convinced that I had been creating mystery and horror instead of being practical and matter-of-fact, as a nurse should. Jason had killed Mrs. Dana, even if he wasn't insanic—and as for the police, they had to be supercareful, naturally.

Betty was looking glum, and I had an idea that she resented my good spirits.

"What's the matter?" I asked. "Anything wrong?"

"Nothing—not a thing," she said peevishly. "I'm merely a young girl chained to the demands of the sick."

"Where did you read that?" I asked, interested.

"Ministering angels," she said bitterly. "Only we're being paid for it, and that puts us out of the amateur or angel class."

"Maybe you saw it in a movie?" I suggested.

"Mind you," she went on, "it's a good profession, and I have nothing against it."

"But—?"

"Yes, but," said Betty and took herself off.

She left some of her dissatisfaction with me. I looked down the familiar corridor, made a face at it, and ardently wished myself in some gay night spot. However, hospital rules had to be obeyed, and the next job was to bed the patients down. I reflected that if it hadn't been a rule I wouldn't bother to bed them down, since they never stayed that way, anyhow. But there were not so many left, and no new patients had come in, so that it did not take long.

Mr. Thomas was in good spirits and said cheerfully, "I feel very well, really—very well. I'll be mighty glad to get home and see my kiddies."

I murmured, "That'll be nice," and tried to keep my mind on what he was saying so that I could make the correct responses.

Mrs. Evans said, "It's absurd, the way they try to keep everything secret in a hospital. I do think you might tell me just what happened about Mrs. Dana."

"There's nothing to tell," I said, lying in the line of duty and hoping it would stick. She was not satisfied, but I managed to get out without giving anything away.

Ad Miller asked, "Why do you attend to the others first? You know I always like to get to bed early."

"Pity, isn't it?"

"I had a very social afternoon," he said wryly. "Out in the solarium, you know—Mrs. Evans and Mr. Thomas. And you can believe this or believe it not, but Mrs. Evans' seven-year-old daughter is in the same grade at school as Mr. Thomas' Junior, who is nine. Mr. Thomas claimed a foul on account of Junior having been out of commission one year with a broken leg, but Mrs. Evans pointed out—and rightly—that that accounts for only one year."

"Fascinating," I said. "I'm absolutely holding my breath."

"I was holding my ears," he told me grimly.

I went on to William Dana, who was lying quietly, looking at nothing.

"How are you feeling?" I asked gently.

"Not so good, Nurse—not at all good. There's no air in here; I've been in this stifling room all day. They took the others out to that sun parlor, but the nurse wouldn't let me go."

I said, "I'm sorry, but they're all scarlet-fever patients, you see."

"I don't care—if I could just get out of this heat. And then Aggie—"

I felt sorry for him and tried to make him as comfortable as possible. But the heat seemed to be worse than ever, and when I got out into the corridor again I wondered how I was going to stand it myself.

Inspector Millard Shaw was waiting for me at the desk, and I had a cold conviction that he was not satisfied with Jason and was looking around for somebody else.

He gave no hint of anything of the sort, however. He asked me a lot of questions and seemed particularly interested in the chair chopping. I told him everything that I knew about it, and after a while he thanked me and said it was only for the record, anyway. He added that he was leaving a man downstairs for a few days, just to make sure that everything went off all right.

After he had gone I considered the man downstairs for a moment. "Very convenient," I thought. "After I'm murdered I can phone down for him to come up."

I was busy for a while and I did not hear the elevator or notice Gavin Bart when he came into the wing. He said, "Hello," as I came hurrying out of the kitchen and scared me almost speechless.

"I'm sorry, I didn't mean to startle you."

"It's all right," I said, catching up on my breathing. "I suppose you want to see your uncle."

"I think I should. How is he taking it? I'm afraid it must have been quite a blow to him."

"Well, yes—"

"I can't understand how it could have happened," he said, staring into space. "Surely some doctor must be badly at fault for not having locked that man up sooner."

I said nothing, but I felt a fresh rush of guilt for my own responsibility in the matter.

We were silent for a moment, and then down the corridor somewhere a man screamed shrilly.

CHAPTER 14

I LEFT Gavin and ran. I thought the sound had come from William Dana's room and I found him at his window, apparently staring out at the floor of the corridor. I hurried in to him and began to urge him back to bed while I spoke soothingly to him. He was quiet while I fussed around making him comfortable, and then suddenly he spoke.

"It's Aggie," he said. "She's here."

"Here?" I stammered and swallowed a mouthful of air. He was looking at me, and I managed to pull myself together and speak as I thought a nurse should.

"Now, Mr. Dana, don't talk nonsense. I expect you've been having nightmares."

He moved his head from side to side and muttered, "No—no, I haven't. She always said she'd come back, but I never believed in it. Always said I didn't think people could come back after they had died. But she has— she left a sign."

"What sign did she leave?"

He opened his mouth to reply and then closed it again and turned his head away. After a moment he said faintly, "Never mind—you'd only think it was silly. It was nothing. I'm quite all right now, Nurse. If you'll just leave the light on when you go out."

He closed his eyes as though he were sleeping, and after a moment's indecision I decided not to disturb him with further questioning. I turned to leave and almost bumped into Gavin, who was standing directly behind me.

I released some of the nervous irritation that I had been bottling up and told him in no uncertain terms all about the rules that forbade visitors in the patients' rooms.

He shrugged and said indifferently, "So what if I catch German measles?"

"I wouldn't care if you caught the black plague," I said crossly. "It's what I'll catch if you're seen in here that worries me."

He smiled then and said, "Listen, sugar, if they treat you badly just tell me and I'll come and tear the place apart."

"Big words," I said briefly. "Too big to mean anything."

I had to scrub him out as well as myself, and I did not take a full breath until we were both safely out into the corridor again.

I remembered that William had seemed to be staring at the floor outside his room, and although the corridor appeared to be the usual expanse of scrubbed, rubberized flooring I lingered for a while and examined it closely.

I found nothing but a small splash of water starring out into tiny rivulets. It could not have been more than half a glassful, and I looked at it, frowning, and wondering how it had come there and if it could possibly have scared William. Certainly there was nothing else on the floor, but how could a small splash of water possibly frighten a man into screaming?

I gave a vexed sigh and wiped the thing up. Gavin, leaning against the wall, watched me with one eyebrow elevated. "Are you taking exercises," he asked presently, "or is there a spot of dirt there not visible to the naked eye?"

I explained about the water and asked if he knew of any reason why it should scare his uncle.

He said, "Good God, no! Why would it? Of course he doesn't like water. What right-thinking citizen does?"

I gave it up and merely asked him if he had spilled the water himself, but he denied any knowledge of it.

We went back to the desk, and Gavin asked casually if Linda was due to appear soon.

I nodded. "Unless she has been excused because of her aunt's death."

"I'll wait around," he decided. "She might come on, and I wanted to see her."

"You could get in touch with her in any case," I suggested.

He nodded vaguely and said, "I suppose so," without stirring. I could see that he was thinking of something else, so I left him to it and got on with my work.

Linda showed up after a while with every blonde curl in place and looking as trim as usual. "Miss Fane said I could be excused," she explained, "but I just felt that I had to work and work hard. And, anyway, I've been worried about Uncle William."

"I think he's all right now," I said doubtfully and proceeded to tell her about what had happened.

"Oh, dear," she wailed. "What on earth is the matter with him?"

"He's had a shock," I said sensibly. "What do you expect, anyway? Your cousin is here, by the way. He wants to see you."

I looked around, but Gavin seemed to have disappeared. "He must be around somewhere," I said, getting up. "I'd have heard the elevator if he'd gone."

We found him at last in the diet kitchen, observing the sink.

"What are you doing here?" I asked in the voice of authority.

"Looking at the sink and wondering how they whip you girls into keeping it so dismally immaculate. It would be cozier with a few coffee grounds lying around the drain." He glanced over my shoulder at Linda and said casually, "Hello."

Linda raised one shoulder, half turned away, and said, "Hello," with frost on it.

Gavin pulled his coat collar up around his neck. "All right, I get it. But I think we ought to stick to a surface civility at a time like this."

She shrugged and said indifferently, "I don't care, as long as you don't speak to me unless it's necessary."

As we left the kitchen and went back to the desk I heard Gavin murmur, "Why would I bother?"

Linda and I had a brief business talk, and then I left while Gavin called after me, "Don't be too long—I'm afraid of being alone with Linda."

I went down to the nurses' dining room, where I saw Miss Fane, who hailed me immediately. I automatically straightened cap and apron, but she had something else on her mind. "You spoke to me about two chairs drawn up to a window in the solarium on your floor," she said in a low voice. "I spoke to the porter, and he says the solarium was cleaned as usual and everything left in its place. He is quite certain that there were not two chairs together at one of the windows and that the light was turned out. So it seems somebody must have come up there and used the place, and I want to find out about it if possible. Have you ever seen any of the girls there when they were off duty?"

I said no with ready emphasis and made no mention of the fact that I had been snatching some sleep there myself when the chair had been chopped up. No one had thought of asking me what I was doing in the solarium on that occasion, and I had volunteered nothing and kept out of trouble.

Miss Fane sighed. "The police declare that they did not leave the light on or disarrange the chairs, but somebody must have done it." She was silent for a moment, her forehead creased in a worried frown, and then her eyes refocused on me, and her voice became brisk. "Oh, and, Miss Gale, pay no attention to Mrs. Evans' talk of someone walking in a vacant room. I'm afraid she finds it necessary to complain about something, even if she has to make it up as she goes along."

She dismissed me, and I made my way to one of the tables and sat down.

When I had finished my meal I went out and was headed for the nurses' home, when I realized that it was considerably cooler outside than in any of the buildings. I lingered on the pathway and thought of Dr. Lawrence, who could lie on the lawn in broad daylight, and from there it did not take me a minute to decide that I could lie on the lawn in the darkness, when no one could see me.

I found an inconspicuous spot which was well shielded by shrubbery and stretched out, feeling deliciously cool and relaxed. I remember noticing a star or two, and then I went into a deep, heavy sleep.

Something disturbed me eventually, and I came awake with a confused idea that there were two men on the other side of the shrubbery. I lay still for a moment, until my head cleared, and then I cautiously raised myself on my elbow and had a look.

Dr. James Lawrence and Gavin Bart were standing together, and I heard Gavin say, "I'm sorry, but you're wrong. I searched the entire floor, and very definitely it is not there."

CHAPTER 15

I MUST have made some sort of noise, because they both turned as one man and saw me. They made no comment while I scrambled to my feet and brushed bits of grass and twigs from my dress, but while I was trying to restore my cap to its place on the back of my head Dr. Lawrence observed impersonally, "It's that raw material from the psychopathic ward."

Gavin laughed shortly. "I think it's been eavesdropping."

"I didn't hear from the beginning," I said, too curious to be tactful. "Would you mind going back and starting all over again?"

"Not at all," Dr. Lawrence said courteously. "Let me see now, Gavin, I believe I started the ball rolling by asking you where you bought your suit—with a preface, of course, to the effect that I just love it."

Gavin nodded. "And I told you I bought it at Chez Macy."

"Right. After which I replied that personally I always trade at Chez Gimbel."

"When I'm able to stop laughing," I said, "maybe you'll tell me what you're looking for. I might be able to find it for you."

They said no almost in unison, and I shrugged and tried to look at my wristwatch. What I almost saw started me toward the hospital on the run.

As I neared the building I realized that they were right along with me, keeping abreast of me in an easy walk.

"What were you doing, skulking around the grounds like that?" Dr. Lawrence asked.

"I was gathering nuts for the winter," I said.

As we were entering the hospital Gavin tapped Dr. Lawrence on the shoulder and said, "Don't go in yet. I have an idea."

The doctor nodded, winked at me, and said, "See you later, snazzy—the gent has an idea."

They turned away, and I raced up to my wing, where I found Linda looking decidedly sour. "Late," she said shortly.

"Sorry," I murmured. "I was talking with two men."

"Oh well"—she relented visibly, which I had counted on—"in that case, of course— Who were they?"

"Nobody you care about," I said, trying to be careless.

"Tell me," said Linda ominously.

I told her and added, "Just because you're through with both of them doesn't make them any the less men. Attractive men, too."

"They are men," she admitted, exhibiting a stern sense of justice, "but as for being attractive—!"

I brushed it aside. "Listen, Linda, what was Gavin searching for while I was away?"

"Why, nothing."

"Were you here at the desk all the time?"

"No, of course not," she said indignantly. "I had work to do in the room."

"The room," I repeated. "Yes, I see. Did the other patients behave themselves and keep quiet?"

Linda said, "Yes," rather absently and with a faraway look in her eye.

"How long were you in there?"

She came back to me with a start and tried to cover up by feigning surprise. "In there? Where? What do you mean?"

"How long was Gavin alone?" I asked impatiently.

"Oh. Not long—not long at all. Well, I'm off now. G'by."

I clutched frantically at her dress. "Wait a minute! Are you and Gavin still at odds—or did you speak to each other?"

"We didn't speak one word to each other after you left," she said emphatically. "That's why I had to go into the rooms. It was too unpleasant with Gavin sitting here at the desk."

She went off, and I sat down and wondered helplessly what Gavin had been searching for that Dr. Lawrence knew about and what was going on, anyway? Jason was under lock and key, certainly, but the wing was not yet back to normal.

I looked down the dim, quiet corridor and wondered how I could possibly spend the remainder of the night there, with four sick people for whom I was directly responsible, and no one to keep me company and tell me not to be a fool when I felt frightened. I had my hand on the phone, determined to call Miss Fane and ask for extra help, and then somehow I couldn't. In the first place, I hated to admit that I was such a sissy, and secondly, I knew Miss Fane would be annoyed, and I valued her good opinion. So I placed my chair with its back to the wall and sat up very straight, straining my eyes down the corridor. Only that didn't work very well, because I began to expect ghosts to come out of the rooms.

It was almost a relief when William Dana's light went on and I was forced into activity.

William was sitting on the side of his bed. He looked up quickly when I came in, but he did not say anything.

"Hadn't you better lie down and try to sleep?" I asked gently.

"No." He dropped his eyes to the floor. "No, I can't. I can't stay here, Nurse. I'm frightened. They'll have to let me go. I—this is like a prison. I can't stand it.

"It isn't so long now before you'll be discharged," I said soothingly.

"But I can't wait—don't you understand?" His voice rose a little. "I'm going now. You'll have to get me my clothes."

"I'll phone down," I said, deliberately vague.

His eyes darted at me suspiciously. "What for?"

"For your clothes, of course."

"Aren't my clothes up here?" he asked desperately.

"Patients are not allowed to bring clothes in with them," I reminded him. "Someone will have to bring them from your home."

"The whole thing is ridiculous," he fumed, half crying. "They came to the house, there, and took all my own clothes off and put me into a pair of hot pajamas two sizes too big for me, and then I had to get into an ambulance. And I'm no more sick than you are." He blinked his eyes excitedly and then gave me a crafty look. "If you—phone downstairs, they won't let me go, will they?"

"I don't know," I said truthfully, "but I'll try, if you like."

He sagged down onto the bed and after a moment's silence said wearily, "Yes, try, please. I'll wait here. Get my clothes if you can—I've got to get out of here."

I went back to the desk and put in a call for Miss Anderson. It was her job, not mine, to tell patients off, and I felt pretty sure that William would be told there was nothing doing about going home.

I perched on my chair again and tried to forget about ghosts emerging from the rooms. "At least," I thought feverishly, "Miss Anderson will be here soon, and I won't be alone."

She showed up within ten minutes, and I told her about William. I went on to explain that he couldn't get out to the solarium during the day and gave it as my opinion that that was what made him so restless. All of which made me feel very like Morgue.

Miss Anderson went straight down to William's room and disappeared within. She was not gone long, and when she reappeared she seemed to have been blown out of the room, while William, unseen, but vociferous, hurled invective after her.

She washed her hands and returned to the desk, looking somewhat flustered.

"What's the matter with him?" I asked.

"Why, I hardly know." She seemed a little indignant. "I told him he'd have to be patient until the end of his quarantine, and he took it quite well. He seemed disappointed, but he said, 'All right, Nurse.' And then I saw that his thumb was bandaged and I asked him about it."

I laughed. "That's happened to me a couple of times. The bandage hasn't been touched since he came in, and I meant to speak to you about it. But he's so absurdly sensitive on the subject that I've just left it alone."

"Well, I don't know what to do about it," Miss Anderson said, still indignant. "I'll speak to Miss Fane."

She went off after telling me that she figured peace was restored, at least until the morning, and I was alone again.

I sat there, watching the corridor. I gave a fleeting thought to the charts and my report and put it away again, almost idly. Jason was gone, but somehow the horror remained in that corridor, and I felt that I had to watch it or be overwhelmed by my own fear.

Somebody had chopped up a chair, and Jason Caddock had been in bed before it happened and after it happened. There was time for him to have done it, of course, but he'd have had to hide his weapon and be back in bed again within a very few minutes. And where could he have hidden the weapon, anyway? The floor had been searched. I thought of Mrs. Dana and remembered that Jason was supposed to have used an ax from the gardener's tool shed, washed it, and replaced it. I wondered where he had washed it and realized that there must be a faucet out there somewhere, since I had seen the garden being watered with a hose.

That was all right, then, but where had Jason hidden that ax after he had chopped up the chair? I kept coming back to that, and there was no answer that my reason would accept.

Dr. Lawrence and Gavin were looking for something too—not the ax, since that had been found in the gardener's shed—but something else. And why should they be prowling around like bloodhounds when the case was closed?

I rubbed my clenched hand across my forehead and thought again of a maniac, loose in the hospital, who had twice slipped into my wing and

crept out again without being seen. And then I thought of Mrs. Dana singing "John Brown's Body" on the first of each month on her front porch-
and over and over again here in the hospital. Slyly, before I could stop it,
my mind leaped on and pictured Mrs. Dana singing "John Brown's Body"
from a throat and mouth mutilated beyond recognition by an ax.

And then all the lights went out.

I rose stiffly from my chair and backed up slowly until I could feel
the solid wall behind my shoulder blades. I waited with my heart pounding and my ears straining into the silent darkness.

For a while nothing happened, and then, quite distinctly, I heard someone padding up the corridor through the blackness.

CHAPTER 16

THE FOOTSTEPS were advancing toward me with a stealthy, padding sound that was yet quite distinct. I flattened my entire body against
the wall, but it did not occur to me to scream or run; I just stood there and
waited for the end.

The footsteps faltered and stopped, and then I heard the swish of a
door and knew that the prowler had entered one of the rooms. With a
queer, deadly calm I decided that it was Mrs. Evans' room or one close to
hers, and on the tail of that thought came a succession of heavy, dull
thuds and then a splintering crash of wood and more thuds.

My unnatural calm broke, and I could feel horror tingle down into
my finger tips. Mrs. Evans! I stretched my arm for the phone, took a step
forward, and tripped over the chair, and then I froze into stillness again as
I heard the footsteps emerge from the room. But they were retreating
now, and in the end they just seemed to die away. I could not tell whether
they had gone down to the end of the corridor or into another of the rooms.

I fumbled wildly for the phone, and when I spoke my voice sounded
high and shrill and rather silly. I must have been a bit incoherent, because
I was told irritably that they were doing what they could about the lights,
and someone would be sent up as soon as it could be managed.

I dropped the phone into its cradle, began to think of Mrs. Evans, and
picked it up again. I told them plenty that time, and a scared voice promised assistance at once.

I backed up against the wall after that, feeling more dead than alive,
and waited for the footsteps to begin again, but nothing happened until

the lights suddenly went on. I jumped and gasped, and as soon as my eyes focused I crept away from the wall and peered fearfully down the corridor. There was no one in sight, and everything appeared to be normal.

And then Mr. Thomas' light went on.

I didn't go down—I couldn't. I just stood there waiting for someone to come and help me.

I heard the elevator doors after a while, and presently Miss Fane came in, followed by George Moon.

"Now, my dear, what's all this?" Miss Fane asked in a voice of wholesome common sense. "You shouldn't get hysterical just because the lights go out. It's happened before, you know—it happened five years ago. We have our own generating plant, and sometimes—"

"Miss Fane," I broke in unsteadily, "someone walked up the corridor and went into one of the rooms, and I'm afraid—Mrs. Evans—"

I indicated Mrs. Evans' door, and the three of us looked at its polished wooden bottom, and blank windowed top. It appeared to be perfectly normal.

Miss Fane frowned, squared her shoulders, and walked straight into Mrs. Evans' room.

Mrs. Evans had apparently been sleeping, and when she started to give Miss Fane hell I breathed a quick sigh of relief and felt myself relax a little.

Miss Fane was not the type to take hell from anybody, and I heard her tell Mrs. Evans to go back to sleep *at once* and stop getting herself all worked up over nothing. Mrs. Evans shut up like a clam.

George Moon grinned, nudged me, and winked. He whispered that it was no wonder Miss Fane had been made a supervisor and then added sourly, "Not that I like her."

"You don't like anybody," I said, still weak with the relief that Mrs. Evans' voice had brought me. "You must admit that Miss Fane is fair, though."

"I don't care if she's fair or not," George declared. "I don't want nobody to be fair to me—I want to be favored."

Miss Fane finished scrubbing out and asked me if I were satisfied.

"He—it—went into one of the rooms," I said unhappily, "and I know there was some damage done. It might be one of the vacant rooms."

Miss Fane hesitated and then went into the vacant room next to Mrs. Evans and switched on the light. George and I piled in after her with our eyes popping.

The room was quite orderly except for the regulation wicker armchair, and that had been practically demolished. The cushions and arms had been wrecked in the same manner as the chair in the solarium.

Miss Fane was silent for a space, and I thought her shoulders drooped a little, but when she spoke her voice was firm and steady.

"Go down and fetch those policemen up here."

George said, "Yes ma'am," and departed, and Miss Fane and I walked slowly back to the desk.

I noticed that Mr. Thomas' light was still on, and I started down the corridor with an air of having just seen it for the first time. Miss Fane nodded absently, her troubled eyes on the door of the vacant room.

Mr. Thomas was indignant and out of patience. "What's the matter, Nurse? Why did you take so long to answer my light?"

"I'm sorry," I said automatically. "I came as soon as I could."

He made a vexed sound with his tongue and asked, "What happened to the lights? Every light in the place must have been off; I looked out the window, and the other wing was in darkness too."

"Some trouble with the generator," I said, having no idea what I was talking about. "But they fixed it; it's going to be all right now."

"But that's inexcusable in a hospital," he fumed. "It might make all the difference to some poor devil on an operating table."

"Our doctors all carry flashlights," I assured him and wondered whether they really did, and if not, would it be worth anything to me to make the suggestion?

I asked Mr. Thomas if there was anything I could do for him, but he was still muttering about the lights, so I turned to leave.

He called me back and, dropping the irritability from his voice, asked if I'd be kind enough to make his bed. "The heat's so bad I've been tossing around, and it's like a pile of hay."

I saw that it was pretty messy, so I remade it as quickly as I could and left him looking decidedly more comfortable.

I found that the two plainclothes men had arrived from downstairs, and they, Miss Fane, and George Moon were all in the vacant room, staring at the wrecked chair. The policemen were both chewing gum, and when I got close enough I recognized one of them as Benny Phipps.

As I came up they all moved out of the room in a body and made off in the direction of the elevator. I flew after them and panted out a shrill request that they leave somebody with me, just as they were stepping into the cage. They considered it for a moment, and then, without troubling to waste words, with one movement they pushed George out again.

The doors closed, and George shook his fist at their blank surfaces.

"That's not very complimentary to me," I suggested. "Why should you get so mad just because you have to stay on the floor and keep me company?"

"You got the wrong idea," George said seriously as we walked back to the desk. "It's them lousy cops—always tryin' to duck work and heave it onto other guys. I like stayin' with you, but I ain't gettin' paid for poundin' a beat, and why should I do it?"

"Maybe you ought to try for the police force," I said idly. "The uniform would be vastly becoming."

"Listen," said George, "what would I do with my fancy stickpin and that collar button my first wife give me—wearin' a uniform?"

He laughed for quite some time over that and was still giving it a reminiscent chuckle now and then when Dr. Lawrence walked into the wing.

George's face froze, and he gave the doctor a cold look.

"Where were you going, George?" Dr. Lawrence asked mildly.

George said, "Nowhere," belligerently.

"Good," said Dr. Lawrence, "then go there, please, right away. I have some private matters to talk over with the student."

"I was told to stay here," said George through clenched teeth. He walked a few feet down the corridor, came back again, and then walked off once more. Over his shoulder he passed the remark that he'd remain out of earshot, but no one was going to make him desert his post.

Dr. Lawrence turned to me and asked pleasantly, "How are you?"

"I'll tell you when I have more time. What is it you want to discuss privately?"

"Nothing," he said, eying my hair. "It seemed a shame to have George hanging around ruining our conversation."

"You mean you came up here in the small hours of the morning just to converse with me?"

He shook his head. "You're hardly that good. I came to look after you and my patient. Somehow, I don't like the feel of the corridor."

"I don't like it either," I said with feeling. "And as for looking after me, you're a bit late. I nearly got beheaded a little while ago, and it wasn't you who saved me—it was all the lights going out."

"What are you talking about?" he asked, his face and voice suddenly serious.

I told him the whole story, and when I had finished he got up abruptly and went straight to the vacant room. I went along with him and noticed that George, standing halfway down the corridor, gave us a severely disapproving look.

Dr. Lawrence and I bent over the chair together and, examining it closely that way for the first time, I saw something that had escaped me before.

It was a small ridge of dried blood.

CHAPTER 17

THE DRY, dark brown ridge lay along the edge of one of the gashes, and I pointed it out excitedly to Dr. Lawrence.

He leaned over and examined it, and then said doubtfully, "How do you know it's dried blood?"

"Well, it looks like it, doesn't it? I've seen dried blood before."

"It also looks like dried mud," said Dr. Lawrence, but he took an envelope from his pocket and scooped some of the stuff into it. "Anyway, we'll find out—and leave some, of course, for the police to play with."

We turned to leave the room and met Benny Phipps coming in at the door. He gave us a bleak, suspicious look and asked, "What are youse doing here?"

"Just looking, thanks," said Dr. Lawrence amiably. "If we decide to buy anything we'll let you know."

Benny's brow darkened. "You ain't supposed to come in here. No one ain't."

Dr. Lawrence turned back and indicated the remaining scrap of blood. "Point that out to the boss, Phipps—it may be worth a promotion to you."

"You go and play marbles with all your little pink pills," Benny said sourly. "I'm takin' care of my own promotions."

We left him there to stew and went on back to the desk, where Dr. Lawrence said with sudden briskness, "I think I'll be getting along. The inspector is due to show up before long, and he'll want to know what I'm doing here if he sees me. I could tell him that I'm a lovesick calf, but it might prove embarrassing. So until tomorrow at about two—same place. Good-by."

He had gone before I could ask him if he were dating me or merely talking, as usual, but I decided that it didn't matter, anyway, and sat down at the desk to do some work.

George Moon was still lingering halfway down the corridor, and after a while Benny stuck his head out of the vacant room and asked George what he thought he was hanging around for.

"I been ordered to stay here," George snarled, "and if the orders is changed I'd like it in writin' or vocal words—if that ain't too much trouble. Because I ain't been doin' so well with my mind readin' just recent."

"In vocal words, then," said Benny out of the corner of his mouth, "get the hell outa here, and go about your business—if you got any."

George turned and came toward the desk with a dark scowl on his face. He slowed to a stop in front of me and demanded to know if this was a democracy or if this was not a democracy. "Because if it is," said George, "we got to do something about the police force. The only real way to tell a democracy is how the police behave."

Benny poked his head out of the vacant room again at this point, and George departed in a bit of a hurry.

I rested my head on my hands for a moment and thought about that ridge of dark dried blood. I felt that it must have come from the weapon which killed Mrs. Dana, which meant that it was still hidden somewhere close by and had never been cleaned. I shivered and raised my head and wondered suddenly if the rest of the patients were all right. The thought sent me down the corridor in a mild panic. Ad Miller's face was pressed against his window, and he tried to entice me in, as usual, but I paid no attention to him. I supposed he had not been awake for long, since his signal light was not yet on, but he was not chopped up in any way, and I went in to William Dana's room without another glance at him.

William had been sleeping, but he stirred when I came in and mumbled, "What's the matter, Nurse?"

His bed was pretty much messed up, so I straightened him out and told him to go back to sleep, but he was staring at the ceiling when I left, and I felt a bit guilty at having disturbed him.

I went to Mr. Thomas' room, found him unscarred and in one piece, and was able to tiptoe out without waking him.

I headed back again with my mind relieved, but when I came to Ad Miller's room his signs became so frantic that I detoured and went in.

"What's going on now?" he asked at once. "I saw you go into those two rooms, and both their signal lights were out. What were you doing?"

"I forgot to kiss them good night," I said, beginning to edge toward the door. "I wanted to see if they'd cried themselves to sleep."

"Orders are still that the patients are to be told nothing," Ad said slowly. "All right, I suppose I can't drag it out of you, but I think I'll write to my congressman. Something happens to Mrs. Dana—police in and out of the place—and I have to sit here twiddling my thumbs and wondering if I'll be next. I don't like it and I'm not sure that I have to put up with it."

"Suppose you go back to bed and stay there until you find out," I suggested.

He flung himself onto the bed, folded his arms behind his head, and narrowed his eyes at me. "Something fresh broke tonight, and don't think I don't know it. I happened to be asleep for a change, but I woke up in time to see George hanging around out in the corridor. Still looking for that bulky formula, perhaps." He frowned, kicked the sheet off, and said, "Come on, honey, be a sport and tell me."

I said, "No," closed my ears to him, and left him still hurling questions.

Mrs. Evans' light was on, so I sighed, made a face at it, and went into her room.

She was sitting bolt upright, perspiring and indignant. "Girl," she said fiercely, "phone my husband! Go and phone him at once. I am leaving this place as soon as I can be helped into my clothes. Rioting in the hall all night, and no suitable explanation—not even an apology. And then that man in the room next door pacing up and down until I feel as though he were walking across my brain."

"Is it the same man who was pacing before?" I asked curiously.

"I don't know. What does it matter? You go and phone my husband right away."

"All right," I agreed mildly. "Only you won't be able to go before morning, anyway—too dangerous in your, condition, you see, so you'd better try to relax and get some sleep in the meantime."

"Well—" She dropped her head back onto the pillow. "I want to get out of here and go home. I'm afraid."

"What are you afraid of?"

But she turned her head to the wall and said, "You go and phone my husband. I'm going home first thing in the morning."

I went out, feeling a bit wobbly about the knees, and stuck my head into the adjacent room.

"Stop pacing around," I said to Benny. "You're disturbing the patient next door."

He removed his toothpick and said, "Ain't that a shame! I'll take my shoes off right away and send some flowers in there in the mornin'."

"Don't be too distressed," I said, eying him coldly.

"If you must move around, just don't use the floor." Benny resumed operations on the toothpick. "You run along, girlie, and attend to your pans, includin' them damn flat ones which are an invention of the devil, and it's a wonder somebody ain't thought of a better system long ago."

I backed out, speechless, and returned to the desk in time to stand at attention for Inspector Millard Shaw, Miss Fane, and Miss Anderson, who came in a procession from the direction of the elevator.

The inspector looked pretty glum and fobbed me off with a brief nod. He went straight to the vacant room, directed by Miss Fane, and proceeded to give Benny a dressing down for having left the room while he went to telephone.

Benny explained that they had left the orderly and added, almost timidly, that it was not a body, but only a mangled chair.

The inspector opened his compressed lips long enough to call Benny a fool and proceeded to an examination of the chair. Benny was silent for a moment, and then his face opened out like a sunflower, and he pointed out what remained of the ridge of dried blood. He had the audacity to announce modestly that he had discovered it himself.

Shaw grunted, examined the particles intently, and finally scraped them into an envelope with a murmured remark to the effect that he would have them analyzed. He turned to Miss Fane then and said that he wanted a thorough search made through the entire hospital for the weapon and added that arrangements would have to be made for his men to go through the patients' rooms. "It must be done as soon as possible," he finished.

Miss Fane looked bothered and said it would be difficult but promised to speak to the superintendent, Dr. Bacon, as soon as she could contact him.

She went off, and Miss Anderson walked back to the desk with me.

Miss Anderson's eyes were very bright, and she had a pretty color in her cheeks. "Isn't it dreadful!" she said excitedly. "It must be a maniac or something. I'm scared to death."

She followed Miss Fane to the elevator, and I sat down and wondered how I was supposed to stand being in sole charge of the wing, when Miss Anderson was scared to death because she had to come there occasionally.

Inspector Shaw departed after a while, leaving Benny on guard. Benny said he was tired, so I locked the vacant room for him, and he went down to the solarium and stretched out on a chaise longue. "And I don't care who was sleepin' here last, girlie," he said with a long sigh. "I don't care if they had smallpox, or what."

I told him not to worry because we always put a ball and chain on the smallpox patients and left him to his slumbers.

I walked slowly back up the quiet corridor and wondered if I'd ever get my routine work finished. I sat down at the desk and made a determined effort, but it wasn't five minutes before I had company again, in the person of Dr. Lawrence. He sat down and looked at me rather soberly across the polished top of the desk.

"I waited until I saw Shaw go," he said rather absently. He seemed to be lost in thought for a moment, and then he spoke again.

"We must find what Mrs. Dana used to call 'my little hatchet.' "

CHAPTER 18

"LITTLE HATCHET?" I whispered. "But that's what they've all been looking for. Why didn't you say something?"

He shrugged. "The place has been searched and nothing of the sort was found—and Gavin didn't want it mentioned. He made his own search tonight, while Linda was on, and found nothing. I met up with him outside after he had finished and when I was on my way up here to watch over you."

I murmured, "Tanks, pal. Whatever would I have done if you hadn't watched over me?"

"You remember," said Dr. Lawrence, "what you are and whom addressing. Gilbert. Act I."

"Act I of what?" I asked.

"Stop interrupting me. As I was saying, I met Gavin outside, and just before you shoved your ear into the proceedings he was telling me that he had searched the entire wing—with the exception, of course, of the occupied rooms—with no result. He had another idea after that, which was to go out to Mrs. Dana's house and search there. I went with him, and we did the place thoroughly, but there was no little hatchet. The nearest thing to it was a big ax out in the garage. Gavin was disappointed and upset, because he's almost afraid to face the fact that she brought her hatchet here to the hospital."

"When did she mention a little hatchet?" I asked curiously. "And why should you be so sure that it's hanging around here?"

Dr. Lawrence shifted restlessly in his chair and squinted thoughtfully at the opposite wall. "I've heard her say, many a time, that she could always protect herself with her little hatchet. I used to laugh at her, but actually she wasn't joking. The last time she referred to it, in my presence, was after she had been admitted here. She said, 'I'll be quite safe because I brought my little hatchet with me.' "

"But that looks as though she had expected trouble," I said slowly. "Either that, or the diagnosis was incorrect and should have been 'barmy in the crumpet.' "

"Miss Gale," said Dr. Lawrence stiffly, "you are out of order."

I said, "Yes sir."

"And anyway," he continued, still squinting at the wall, "I believe that disorders of the kind are now labeled 'insanic' by the more up and coming of our young interns. However, we digress. When Mrs. Dana said she'd brought her hatchet with her I paid no attention to it, because she was always chattering.

"When I remembered it later I mentioned it to Gavin, who admitted that he'd heard her speak of the thing but declared that he had never seen it. He always doubted its existence, in any case—said he thought she was referring to her own tongue, and that's very reasonable too."

"Have you told the police?" I asked.

He shook his head. "I intend to, though, since we were unable to find any hatchet at her house."

"Benny Phipps is down in the solarium," I suggested. "I wouldn't mind waking him for you. I'd love it."

"No," he said, "not Benny. He'd probably arrest me. I'll wait until I meet up with Shaw. In the meantime you might search the patients' rooms—without being too obvious about it."

I pointed out that that had already been done but agreed to try again. He nodded and appeared to go into a brown study, so I turned to my work and attempted to get a little of it done while I had someone to watch over me.

Several minutes passed in silence, and then he spoke again.

"My first idea—to go home and go to bed—was right. I mean when I said same time and place tomorrow and bade you good-by. I'm falling asleep in this chair. Benny has been left here to take care of you, and I can't see any real need for me to sit here and suffer."

"None whatever," I said coldly.

"Good." He stood up and did a little polite stretching. "I like my women to be reasonable."

"Interesting, I'm sure," I said, still chilly, "but nothing to do with me."

"Not necessarily," he agreed, laughing down at me. "But you never know what fate has in store for you. Well, I'll meet you same time and place tomorrow. 'By."

He went off, and as soon as the elevator door had closed on him I was drenched in fear again. I abandoned any attempt to work and sat watching the corridor, with very little more idea of what went on there when my back was turned than had Ad Miller. He seemed to think I could tell him the whole tale, if rules allowed, and yet I knew little beyond what he himself suspected.

I went into the diet kitchen to prepare my coffee, but it was so blank and silent that I came out again in a hurry. I hesitated for a moment and then went down to the solarium.

Benny was stretched on the chaise longue with his eyes wide open. When he saw me he grinned from ear to ear and said, "Fooled you, girlie. You thought I'd be sleepin' on the job, didn't you?"

I said, "Naw. How about a cup of coffee?"

"How about it?"

"I'm going to make some," I explained. "Want a cup?"

"Sure." He heaved himself off the chaise longue and followed me along the corridor. Ad Miller was standing at his window; but I was so bored with his insomnia that I merely made a face at him and passed on.

Benny seemed to have cheered up considerably. He perched himself on a stool while I was preparing the coffee and told me many stories of conquest, Benny being the conqueror.

When he ran down a little I wound him up again by telling him how glad I was that he was there to guard me—and the patients, of course.

He opened up happily at that and told me a little about the present case.

"That guy Caddock, now—the doctors don't think he's a nut, just dumb. My chief ain't satisfied—and me neither. See, the guy chops up the first chair—O.K. Now where does he hide the weapon?" Benny paused, swallowed coffee and added, "Where could anybody hide it, for that matter? The joint searched and everythin'."

"I thought they had found the weapon in the gardener's shed," I murmured.

"Oh, that." Benny shrugged. "Time element. Somebody else could-a used that, but this Caddock guy didn't have no time to put it away. And anyways, this business tonight—that lets Caddock out."

He handed his cup over for more coffee, took a gulp, and shook his head.

"Been a lotta trouble, this case—lotta routine work—tryin' to tie someone up with the Dana dame. But nobody ties—only the brother. We looked 'em all up. That orderly, Moon—he's sweet on you, ain't he?"

"Certainly not," I said with some heat.

Benny appeared to reserve judgment. "All I know, when we questioned him, he says you're in the clear—didn't have nothing to do with it—but there ain't another soul in the whole goddamn joint he give the benefit of the doubt to."

"And you couldn't find anyone who ties up with Mrs. Dana in any way?" I asked, trying to change the subject.

"Nope. Miss Fane, Miss Anderson, Dr. Bacon—"

"Dr. Bacon!" I gasped. "Why, he's the superintendent."

"Sure," said Benny. "We can't leave no stones unturned in a thing like this here. We tried the patients—Mrs. Evans, Mr. Miller, Mr. Thomas—didn't know the old dame, no business dealings."

"What about Linda and Gavin?"

"Niece and nephew," Benny identified them. "We worked on them, but nothin' doin'. They went around there sometimes, but they never gave her no money, and she never gave them none—or not much. Anyways, in their jobs they couldn't give her cash like she lived on."

"Cash?" I repeated curiously.

"Yeah. Funny thing," said Benny, "they didn't have no income, her or the brother, but the old lady had some stocks and bonds piled up for a rainy day."

"What did she live on, though?" I asked.

He shrugged. "She showed up at her bank every month carryin' a small hatful of cash. It wasn't so much, but that's what they lived on."

"What about the dividends from her securities?"

"She piled them up and bought more securities. She wasn't one to throw her nickels away, see? She lived penurious."

"Didn't you find anything at her house? Books or papers that might explain the cash deposits?"

Benny shook his head. "We been over the place from attic to cellar too. But the chief and I are goin' out there again, and we'll tear it apart."

"But there must be some tie-up with somebody," I said helplessly.

Benny abandoned his coffee cup, yawned, and moved his toothpick from his vest pocket to his mouth. "Oh well, we got the niece and nephew, the brother and the doctor. Brother don't work, nephew clerk in an insurance company; niece does nursin'. Doc Lawrence is the only one with money, and he got his from his father when the old man cashed in."

"What!"

Benny nodded.

"Good!" I said. "I didn't know that."

"Ah, nuts," said Benny. "What's money, anyway?"

"Nothing at all," I said. "What about the rest of the patients?"

"Mr. Thomas is a lawyer and does pretty good with it, and the husband of the Evans dame works in a department store for thirty-seven hundred dollars per."

"Per what?"

"Per year, girlie. But the way this Evans dame manages all the pennies, you'd think it was five thousand. The Miller guy ain't so steady—sometimes he's in the chips; sometimes he ain't. Bets on the horses, bit of radio announcing—things like that. He gets along, and he don't seem to be crooked. Anyway, he's never come our way."

I had cleared away the coffee things by that time, and we both moved out into the hall. I glanced down the corridor and noticed almost at once something on the floor that glinted in the subdued rays of one of the footlights that were set low down on the wall on each side of the doors.

I walked slowly down the corridor and stood staring at a small pool of water that lay directly in front of William Dana's door.

CHAPTER 19

I STOOD and looked at that splash of water and felt as though a cockroach were wandering up my spine. I gave my head a quick shake after a moment and crept into William Dana's room. He seemed to be sleeping, and I was able to get out again without disturbing him. I went straight across the corridor to Ad Miller's room and was conscious of Benny watching me idly, thumbs stuck into his waistcoat, and the toothpick moving gently in a rotating motion.

Ad was in bed for a change and actually asleep. He woke up when I came in and squinted at me owlishly.

"Nice timing," he said with a touch of bitterness. "You gave me the brush-off when I begged and pleaded with you to come in earlier, and as soon as I give up and nurse myself to sleep—"

"Listen," I said, "did you spill a glass of water out in the corridor?"

He woke up completely at that and gave me a look of faintly amused astonishment. "Pull yourself together, dear—you're raving. You and I both know that if I so much as set foot in that corridor I'd be arrested."

"So you didn't spill water in the corridor?"

"Don't," said Ad, "take your housekeeping so seriously. If you must have a direct answer—no, I did not spill water in the corridor."

"You were glued to your window most of the evening," I said. "Didn't you see anything? See who spilled the water, I mean?"

"I was not glued to my window, dear," said Ad with mild reproof. "I looked out occasionally to relieve the boredom, but even if I had seen anyone spill water on your sacred floor I wouldn't squeal."

"Please!" I said feverishly. "Stop joking and try to think. Even if you didn't see the water spilled you might have seen someone in the hall who could have done it."

Ad folded his arms behind his head and gave me a charming smile. "Look, sweetie, you go and wipe up that mess and give up all thought of revenge. I saw cops, doctors, nurses, and orderlies in the corridor—and no one else—and undoubtedly one of that number spilled the water, if it was water. How do you know it isn't gin? Have it analyzed, and if it's gin you might narrow the suspects to the cops and the orderly."

I left him, and out in the corridor I took his advice and cleaned up the mess. Benny lounged down and asked what I was doing, so I told him all about it.

He thought it over for a while, hands in his pockets, and rocking from toes to heels. "It's hard to tell," he said presently, squinting into the distance, "whether it was the water scared the old man or not. You should of left this splash here and seen whether it scared him again. He ain't seen it this time, I guess."

He acted on his own suggestion and spilled some fresh water on the spot where I had cleaned it up.

I shook my head in doubt and distaste. "I don't like leaving a mess around, for one thing, and I don't want poor Mr. Dana to be frightened again—he's had enough."

"You leave it," said Benny. "Probably it don't mean a thing, anyway."

"Then why must I leave it?"

"Because," said Benny, "we can't leave no stones unturned. That's the way the police work."

"Yes," I said, heading back to the desk, "and when you're through what do you have? Just a row of stones turned over."

"Are you nuts," asked Benny, "or what?"

I worked hard from then on, and when I went to give the morning wash-ups, I did not forget to look around for Mrs. Dana's little hatchet in each of the patients' rooms.

Mr. Thomas was easy. He never noticed my hasty search, because he kept himself busy and happy talking about his Junior's prowess at football. He was still talking when I left him, and I don't think he even noticed my departure.

Ad Miller caught on at once, of course, but he was not troublesome. He merely wanted to know if I were looking for a gun or a bottle of poison. "I think, in all justice, that you should tell me whether we patients are being murdered off one by one or whether it's a case of theft."

"Don't waste my time," I said coldly. "I know it isn't in Linda to keep anything to herself, and if she hasn't told you all I'll eat my cap."

"All very true," he agreed, quite without embarrassment, "but Linda is inclined to garble things—and anyway, something else happened tonight, and I'd love to know what it is."

"You'll have to wait for Linda's garbled account," I said shortly.

When I searched Mrs. Evans' room she noticed it at once and said, "Stop snooping, girl!"

I stopped because I had finished, anyway, and Mrs. Dana's little hatchet was not there.

Mrs. Evans was full of complaints about the bad night she had put in. "I had always supposed that a hospital was a sanctuary for peace and quiet—but not this one. No sir."

"Oh, come, now," I said absently. "It's not as bad as all that."

"No," Mrs. Evans agreed fiercely. "It's worse."

I went on to William Dana's room and stepped right into the puddle of water. I went in, after calling Benny an addle-pated fool, and found William sleeping peacefully. I hated to wake him, but I told myself grimly that the hospital must go on, and set to work.

William opened his eyes and said almost at once, "I have a headache, Nurse."

I murmured something soothing, and he lay passive while I fixed him up. He did not seem to notice when I made my brief search, and it could not have been very noticeable in that small, rather bare room, but where the other patients had had no personal possessions, William had his sister's carpetbag lying in a corner, and I knew that I should look through it. I opened it swiftly, and after rifling through the papers I was satisfied that there was no hatchet in among them.

Just before I straightened my aching back William's voice, shrill and angry, beat me about the ears.

"Nurse, Nurse, what are you doing? Get out of that bag—get out at once! You've no right—no right whatever—"

I had finished, anyway, so I closed the bag, apologized, and murmured a silly remark about having dropped something into it.

His eyes widened, and his voice dropped to a whisper. "You mean it was open?"

I looked at him in some surprise. The bag had been closed but not locked, but if I admitted that I'd have to admit having opened it. "It was slightly open," I said and felt ashamed of myself.

I could see his thin throat ripple as he swallowed convulsively, and he turned his head to the wall and closed his eyes.

I went out, feeling troubled and dissatisfied, and stepped into the puddle again. It was smeared all over the floor by this time, so I wiped the whole thing up in a fit of angry impatience.

Benny was sitting in a chair by the desk, and when I told him what I had done he grunted without moving. I looked at him curiously and could have sworn that he was sound asleep with his eyes open. And yet it didn't seem possible, and when Betty appeared I asked her what she thought.

"I believe it can be done," Betty said. "I think I've heard of such cases."

She leaned over and peered into Benny's face, but Benny kissed her, said, "Thank you, girlie," and stood up and stretched.

Betty tightened her mouth into a thin line. "God help all women," she said. "What's he doing here, anyway? Something new?"

I told her all about it and presently left her with her face rather white and muttering things like, "Impossible—no sense to it—absolutely crazy—screw loose—"

I went down to breakfast and found Linda there looking moody and unhappy.

"They questioned me," she wailed. "Questions and questions—I don't know whether I'm coming or going. They're going to search the whole darned hospital this morning. Dr. Bacon is going with them. That Shaw man says it must be found."

"It?" I asked, sipping coffee.

"The ax."

"How do you know it's an ax?"

"Well, I don't. But you have to call it something. Weapon sounds silly."

"Linda," I said suddenly, "did you ever hear your aunt speak about something that she called her 'little hatchet'?"

Linda stared at me, her forehead drawn into a puzzled frown, and then suddenly her fork dropped with a clatter onto her plate, and she got up and left without a word.

CHAPTER 20

I LEFT what remained of my breakfast and ran after Linda. I knew that it was important to catch up with her quickly, because she never could keep anything to herself, and the chances were that she'd spill whatever information she had to the next person who crossed her path.

I went out into the grounds and saw her heading for the nurses' home, but at the same time Miss Fane and Inspector Millard Shaw hove into view, apparently coming away from the nurses' home, and they caught her first. The inspector asked her something, and she answered impatiently just as I came abreast of the group. I drifted to a stop with my ears flapping, but it turned out to be a fatal mistake. Shaw gave Linda a nod that released her and turned on me with a barrage of questions. It seemed to me that he repeated each question at least six times, and I answered mechanically and truthfully, too, while I kept one eye on the doorway of the nurses' home into which Linda had disappeared.

It must have been nearly half an hour before Shaw dismissed me, and as soon as I was free I made a beeline for Linda's room. I met her coming out of it arrayed in a linen dress of a soft chartreuse green with a matching wide-brimmed straw hat.

I admired the costume with one corner of my mind even while I was saying breathlessly, "Wait, Linda, where are you going?"

She gave me a cold look which I recognized as her defense against people to whom she feared she was about to give something away. She said, "Nowhere in particular," and tried to brush past me.

I hung onto her and asked, "Have you given up sleeping?"

"Don't be silly."

"Then why don't you sleep first, so that you'll be fresher for wherever you're going?"

She avoided my eye and said, "No, I'd better go now."

"Can't you tell me where you're going?" I persisted.

"I'm just going out to the house. Let me past, Norma—I want to get started."

I stood my ground and said persuasively, "Now, wait a minute. Why don't you let me go with you? You know I'd like to help you—you've been through a bad time."

The hostility went out of her, and she pulled off her hat and fingered its sweeping brim in a troubled fashion. "I really don't know what to do. It's kind of awful, I guess. Maybe—well, come on into my room and I'll tell you about it. I feel like a wreck, anyway."

I followed her, feeling faintly guilty at having taken advantage of a human sieve, and we sat down and pulled out cigarettes.

Linda exhaled smoke in a thin, firm stream, absently flicked ashes onto the floor, and said slowly, "I never paid much attention to Aunt Aggie; she was always talking in riddles and stuff like that—she loved to talk, anyway. But when you mentioned that little hatchet I remembered something she'd said the first night she was here. She was chatting along the way she usually did, and then right in the middle of it she said, 'My little hatchet is both literal and figurative. We won't talk about the literal, but the figurative is interesting. It actually has power to kill, but it's safely put away in my house. Two flights up and three flights down in the northeast corner, but you wouldn't be able to figure it out, anyway.'

"She started scolding me then because she said there was an uncomfortable lump in the mattress."

We both smoked in silence for a space while I thought it over.

"So you're going right out to her house and try to follow directions," I said presently.

Linda nodded.

"Let me go with you," I said eagerly. "Only let's go this afternoon. We're both too tired now; we wouldn't be able to do anything. We'll sleep first, and then maybe we'll be fresh enough to discover something."

She agreed listlessly, and I could see that she had lost her first enthusiasm. However, I made a date with her for two o'clock and went off to my own room, asking myself what business it was of mine. And answer came there none.

There is one thing about slaving in a hospital: you work so hard and long that you have no time to fool around with insomnia or toss feverishly on a hot pillow. My pillow was hot enough, but when my alarm clock went off at ten to two my head was exactly where I had put it at eight-thirty.

I slipped into a thin pale blue dress with white daisies on the pockets, ran a comb through my hair, and hurried over to Linda's room. She had double-crossed me and was still sound asleep, so I woke her up ruthlessly. I was feeling the excitement of the chase, or something, and I was eager to be off.

Linda had lost all her enthusiasm by this time, and she squirmed away from me, muttering, "Don't let's bother—there's nothing in it. Aunt Aggie always talked through her hat."

I persisted grimly, however, and managed to get her dressed and out of the building.

As we walked toward the street I caught sight of Dr. Lawrence in a distant part of the grounds and decided that he must have been serious about our two o'clock date. I smirked, and Linda noticed it. "What's the matter with you?" she asked crossly. "You look like a cat with a saucer of cream."

"You're not kidding," I said briefly.

We had to take a bus to the Dana house, and when we arrived in the district I noticed that it was rather sparsely settled. There was an occasional malignant growth of little new houses with large, shabby, old-fashioned places dotted here and there.

Mrs. Dana's house was one of the old ones—medium-sized, with two main stories, an attic and a cellar. There was a front porch with several weather-beaten steps leading up to it, and on the house itself two parasitic growths of bay windows. The street was short, with only four houses on the Dana side and two opposite.

As Linda and I approached I noticed a man standing on one of the flower beds and leaning against the porch. He appeared to be peering at the sky. I put a hand on Linda's arm, and we slowed to a stop.

"What's he looking at?" Linda said and glanced up at the sky. "Oh, I see. It's going to rain."

"Come back to earth," I muttered. "Do you think, he's a cop?"

"No, of course not," Linda said, surprised. "Cops have to wear uniforms."

"Oh, please!" I said in disgust. "Go back to the kindergarten and get an education."

"It is going to rain," she declared. "I'm so glad. Maybe it will break the heat."

"Listen," I said, pinching her. "Are there any side entrances so that we can get in without that fellow seeing us?"

"Side door?" said Linda. "Yes, of course. She always made us use the side door so that we wouldn't track up the porch."

"Have you a key for the side door?"

"Why, no—she used to leave the door open, mostly."

I think I snarled at that point. "It will certainly be locked now, anyway. Why do you come out on a wild-goose chase like this without any sense to it?"

"Well, I like that!" Linda wailed. "I said I didn't want to come. I told you I'd changed my mind—"

I took hold of her arm and cut her short. "Come on, we'll walk up the path of the house next door and around to the side. Then we can cross over to your house without him seeing us."

She followed me, saying in a complaining voice, "It isn't my house. I suppose Gavin will get it eventually. I don't suppose she left me anything."

The man eyed us once or twice but made no move as we disappeared between the two houses. We slipped across to the side door of Mrs. Dana's house and found the door locked, as I had supposed.

"Oh, dear," Linda said dispiritedly. "I guess we'll just have to go back."

"Don't be a sissy. This is an ordinary old-fashioned lock, and I have my own back-door key. Maybe it will fit."

It did too. We slipped in the side door half a minute later, and just as the first drops of rain were falling.

The house was hot and oppressive with stale air, and the furniture was nondescript and old-fashioned. Linda led me through the kitchen, dining room, and living room, and toward the stairs. "Up two flights and down three," she murmured, starting up.

I said, "Hey! Wait a minute. Why don't we just go down the cellar? Or do you need the exercise?"

"No," said Linda. "We don't just go down cellar—that's not what she said. It was up two flights and down three."

"I guess I'm just dumb," I said and grimly followed her up to the second floor.

Four rooms opened from a square of center hall, and I asked, "Whose bedroom was whose?"

"Aunt Aggie's bedroom in the front," Linda replied, "Uncle William in the back, and the two smaller rooms in between are Aunt Aggie's sewing room and the guest room."

The floor of the hall was plain dark varnished wood, but directly in front of Uncle William's room was a large spot where the wood was lightish and the varnish had worn off.

CHAPTER 21

LINDA HAD started up the attic stairs, but I remained staring at the discolored floor outside William's bedroom.

Linda called, "Come on," and I yelled, "What's this?" at the same time, and neither of us received an answer. I could hear Linda carefully turn herself around in the attic and start down the stairs again still methodically following instructions. I waited until she reappeared in the hall and then asked, "Linda, what's the matter with the floor here in front of your uncle's room?"

She spared it a glance and said impatiently, "I don't know. What difference does it make? Come on, we have to go down two more flights."

"Doesn't it look as though water had been spilled here?" I said, not moving.

"Yeah. Come on, can't you?"

"But isn't that strange? Don't you remember? I told you at the hospital about that water."

But Linda had gone on down the stairs, and I followed her slowly. I was trying to reason the thing out calmly and logically, but there just did not seem to be any logical explanation of the fact that water was always spilled in front of William Dana's bedroom, no matter where his bedroom happened to be.

I followed Linda to the cellar and was in time to hear her let out a squeaky exclamation.

"Norma, look! Somebody's been here. They've torn the place apart."

I pushed past her and looked around the dim, dusty place. The cellar was fairly small, but directly in front of us a great gap had been torn in the wall. We moved forward together and poked our heads gingerly into the hole.

We saw a room which had been walled away from the main basement and was crammed with a number of curious-looking objects which meant nothing to me until Linda gasped, "It's a still! Can you imagine a thing like that? Aunt Agnes running a still! She never touched a drop, either—used to turn up her nose at the stuff."

I knew that Linda often got things mixed up, and I asked doubtfully, "How do you know it's a still?"

"I had a boyfriend who ran one—he was a sheriff—and he showed it to me."

"If he showed it to you," I said politely, "he was an utter fool as well as a sheriff, and I'll bet any amount you care to name that he ended up in the clink."

Linda said, "What's that?" vaguely, and I murmured, "Who broke the wall down?"

"How should I know?" said Linda.

"Well, I do," I said thoughtfully. "It was the police, of course. That's why they have a man outside."

We became conscious of rain beating against the small dusty windows. There was no thunder or lightning, but a steady downpour, and Linda glanced up and said, "Poor Uncle William—he hates rain."

"He hates rain?" I repeated slowly.

"Uh-huh. Now listen, Norma, where's the northeast corner?"

"He hates rain," I went on, talking more to myself. "Maybe he hates water in general."

"Where's north from here?" Linda was saying. "For that matter, where's east?"

I opened my mouth to tell her and had to close it again when I realized that I did not know. "I can't do all the headwork," I said instead. "Weren't you ever a Girl Scout?"

"What's that got to do with it?"

"I'd know my directions if I were at the hospital," I said helplessly. "But here I'm all turned around."

"Oh, dear," Linda mourned. "We might just as well go back and give up."

"Don't be silly. We'll simply have to look in all the corners."

"Oh, sure, of course. Come on, let's look in the brewery first."

"Brewery!" I murmured, raising my eyebrows.

However, there was nothing in the brewery that could have been called a figurative hatchet, and Linda, brushing at her dress with dusty hands, was obviously getting tired of the whole thing. "Maybe Aunt Aggie was simply a loony. It makes me feel silly to look for something I don't even know what it is."

"Oh, come on," I said firmly. "Benny says that no stone should be left unturned."

We left the brewery and began to burrow around in the corners of the cellar. I was getting a bit tired of it myself by that time, and I began to feel silly, officious, interfering, and even a little scared. I was nearly ready to give up when I found a photograph frame that had no picture beneath the glass but a square of note paper that was covered with small, neat, evenly spaced writing. I read the first few words which ran, "Life is a strange and dangerous thing—"

I tucked the thing hastily under my arm and called to Linda. "Psst! I think I have it, but we'll have to study it back at the hospital; it's too long to read here. Come on, let's go."

I started up the stairs, and Linda crowded behind me, talking excitedly. "What is it, anyway? Why don't you show it to me? What's all the mystery?"

As we stepped into the kitchen someone opened the front door and walked into the hall.

"Hurry!" Linda hissed and, catching me by the arm, she ran me straight into the pantry and closed the door. Immediately she showed utter dismay. "It's the wrong door," she moaned. "I thought it was the back door."

"Quick thinking," I said bitterly, and at that moment the footsteps pounded into the kitchen. I pushed the pantry door open a crack and peered out in time to see the plainclothes man settle into a chair and hoist his feet onto the kitchen table.

Linda, looking over my shoulder, backed away again with a stricken look and pointed to the tiny window behind us. I glanced at it, looked meaningly at Linda's hips, and shook my head.

"Rubbish!" I said loudly. "Now I'm certain that jam is here somewhere."

Linda's mouth dropped open, and she put her hand on what she used to think was her heart until she took up nursing.

The policeman dropped his feet onto the floor with a bang and flung the pantry door wide. Before he could say anything I gave a little shriek and yelled, "Heavens! Who are you? What are you doing here?"

He seemed a bit taken aback and said almost defensively, "I'm keepin' an eye on the place, lady. I didn't see you come in. I thought you went in next door."

I brushed past him, carrying a pot of jam in my hand. "What do you mean, my good man? Are you of the constabulary?"

His eyes slitted coldly, and he regained some of his aplomb. He said, "Yeah—and who are you?"

"I'm Mrs. Dana's niece. I suppose it's all right for you to come in out of the rain, but please don't damage the furniture. If you get hungry you may try some of the jam—there's more in the pantry. Good day."

I sailed out, and Linda scuttled after me. I glanced back once and saw the cop eying us gloomily from the side door, but he made no move to follow us.

Linda giggled. "You certainly got us out of that mess."

"What do you mean? You have a right to go to your aunt's house."

"Well, sure, except you told him you were the niece. Why did you do that?"

"You looked like my half-wit assistant," I said and added obscurely, "I didn't want him to think I was exploiting the dumb."

"Are you calling me dumb?" Linda asked indignantly.

"No," I said, "you merely act that way. Isn't the rain wonderful?"

We were waiting for the bus, and the soft, steady summer rain poured onto our heads and shoulders with such refreshing coolness that we made no effort to seek shelter.

Once on the bus we dribbled all over the seat and floor, and Linda said fretfully, "Maybe I am dumb, after all—and you too. I feel fit to catch pneumonia."

I gave her the pot of jam and said, "Hang onto that. I'm holding the evidence."

She put the jam onto the floor, and we both pored over the picture frame, but it was impossible to read anything with the bus rattling and jouncing, and we had to put it away again.

It had stopped raining by the time we got back to the hospital, and we went straight to our rooms and changed our wet clothes.

We both piled onto my bed when we were dry once more and studied the framed note.

We couldn't make much out of it. It spoke of life in a lofty, high-flown sort of way, hinted at an anonymous person who was described as dangerous, and boasted briefly that the author could be dangerous, as well. Toward the end it suddenly dropped out of the clouds and stated, "Do not allow my brother William to get hold of my carpetbag under any circumstances whatever."

CHAPTER 22

"OH, GLORY!" Linda moaned. "I took that bag into him myself when he asked for it."

"I guess that makes me an accessory," I said uncomfortably, "be-cause I watched you do it."

"Maybe we'll be arrested," she whispered. "I know I had no right to move the darned thing; I shouldn't have touched anything in that room."

"It's all right," I reassured her. "They haven't found out about it, and if they do we'll say that William was fit to have hysterics and we gave him the bag to keep him quiet. Shaw looked through it, anyway, and there was nothing but those fake securities."

We had to go then, but we hid Mrs. Dana's framed note in the bottom of my bureau drawer first.

When I got to my post I found Betty and Morgue conversing at the desk, and to my surprise I saw that Betty was putting a certain amount of sparkle into it.

They nodded to me as I came up, and Morgue went into his scientific act immediately.

"Mr. Dana," he said, "Mr. William Dana—little trouble there; Miss Gale."

I said, "Yes sir, Dr. Gill," and waited patiently.

"There seems every reason to suspect a phobia," said Morgue, pursing his lips.

I opened my mouth, but he got in ahead of me. "He shows signs of an aggravated fear of rain."

Betty tried to shove her oar in, but Morgue gave her such a look of reproach that she backed quietly out again and let him do the talking.

"He is very definitely under the weather," said Morgue. He let out an unexpected chuckle and then had to explain that it was a joke. Betty kindly gave him a silvery laugh, but I nodded coldly.

Morgue rested his broad shoulders against the wall and put the tips of all his fingers together.

"It seems that rain always upsets him, and, in fact, he has an aversion to water under any conditions. He explains it with an accident in his childhood when he was very nearly drowned."

"He makes no objection to his daily wash-up," I said.

Morgue frowned at the interruption. "He clenched his teeth and endured it, Miss Gale. And anent that daily wash-up—er—it doesn't seem to have been satisfactorily thorough. I discovered—er—well, he has just been thoroughly scrubbed, and what with that and the rain, his condition became such that I was obliged to administer a sedative."

I stared at Morgue and suddenly felt a guilty burning in my face. "Wait a minute—now that I come to think of it, I never did wash him. He offered to do it himself every time, and of course he wasn't really sick, so I let him. I did everything else for him."

"Don't apologize, child," said Morgue, getting really offensive. "I understand, of course. Only you should have realized, after a day or two, that he simply was not washing at all."

"Yes," I said. "Especially in this heat."

"Don't be flippant, Miss Gale, and try to be more careful in the future," said Morgue, having himself a wonderful time. "And don't try to bathe the patient again. I shall arrange to have it done at suitable intervals." He straightened up, removed the brave young scientist from his face, and substituted something that I took to be the tender young lover. "Good night, Betty, have a good sleep."

He walked off with slightly bent head, and I raised my eyebrows at Betty. "Romance is in the air, maybe?"

"Don't be silly," said Betty and added, "He's taking me to a show in New York on my day off."

"Don't let him talk shop," I warned her. "It seems to upset him, and he invents words like 'insanic.' "

"What are you raving about?" asked Betty and presently took herself off.

I settled down to the night's business, but I had not been at it for half an hour when the clang of the elevator doors was followed by quick, staccato footsteps. I stood up at once, feeling both surprised and pleased. I can always recognize Mother's footsteps. She came in, looking trim and brisk as usual, and shook me vigorously by the hand, because, as she put it, kissing was apt to spew germs around.

She sat herself down and motioned me to a chair. "It's nice to see you, Norma, but I'm here to talk to you seriously, with Miss Fane's permission."

I started right then to gird myself, because I knew something was coming up.

"I told Miss Fane I wanted you transferred to another wing," Mother continued, "but she refused point-blank."

I tried not to giggle as I pictured Mother and Miss Fane crossing swords—the irresistible force and the immovable object about summed it up.

"Young girls like you exposed to the sort of thing that has been going on here. I told her I wouldn't have it."

"What did she say?" I asked happily.

"She fobbed me off with some sort of feeble assurance that a policeman was always on guard. I told her it wasn't good enough and that I'd insist on your leaving, even if it meant chucking your profession."

"Mother!" I gasped. I was shaken to the core, as she had always told me that my profession was sacred—don't give up the ship—nor allow snow, rain, or heat of summer to keep me from my appointed rounds.

I gave her a look of shocked reproof, and there was no doubt that she shuffled a little, but she kept her chin up and brazened it out.

"It's not only the police and their pretty uniforms," she said, going off at a bit of a tangent, "but there's that man, Addison Miller—I don't like him. He's nothing but a playboy."

"You needn't worry about him, Mother," I said. "He's not playing with me."

"I'm glad to hear it." She adjusted her hat, recrossed her legs, and avoided my eye by looking down the corridor, and I knew that something else was coming.

"Er—I believe there's a doctor hanging around, too, isn't there?"

"Droves of them," I said carelessly. "The nurses are thinking of taking out accident insurance because we're always stumbling over them."

But Mother was not to be diverted. She stopped looking down the corridor and began to bore holes through me with her eyes. "I'm referring to one doctor in particular."

I never was a match for her and I heard myself saying vaguely, "Well, there's one who hangs around a bit. He sent a couple of patients here."

Mother nodded. "That's the one. He's been courting you, hasn't he?"

"He's been doing nothing of the kind," I said hotly and felt myself blushing.

"Oh yes, he has," said Mother. "I can see it in your face, and anyway, as the girl said in Shakespeare, you're protesting too much."

"What makes you think it was a girl who passed that remark?" I asked sulkily in a futile attempt to change the subject.

"It was a girl—I read all about it in high school. But we're talking about James Lawrence—not Shakespeare."

"Well, what about him?" I asked defiantly.

"He's engaged," said Mother.

I raised my eyebrows, settled my cap, and heard myself saying in a high, squeaky voice, "So what?"

"So don't let him make a monkey out of you. I saw it in this morning's paper. I met Miss Fane in the street yesterday, and she had told me about him. He's marrying a girl by the name of Fish—Louise Fish."

"Well, that's nice for Louise," I said calmly. "I'd step aside for her anyway. She has to get her last name changed, come what may, and I can afford to wait."

Mother stood up and pulled down her girdle.

"I still think you should come home with me right now."

"My head is unbowed," I said, "and it isn't even bloody yet. I shall stick to my post."

It was the sort of thing Mother had always pounded into me, so she had to give up. She said merely, "If I can't move you I suppose I can't, but you be very careful and don't let them leave you in this wing alone."

I promised, and she forgot about the germs and kissed me good-by.

I sat on at the desk after she had gone, wondering in a detached sort of way why Dr. Lawrence didn't spend more time with his Fish. Had I been the Fish, I reflected, I should have been a trifle annoyed.

I glanced down the corridor, but it was too early in the evening for me to be frightened; the fear seemed to come in the small hours of the morning. I got up and walked down to William Dana's room, but a glance at the floor outside showed it to be quite dry.

I thought of William and his abnormal fear of water and wondered if someone in the hospital knew of it, and immediately I was convinced that someone did. I thought it likely that Mrs. Dana had spilled water in front of his door at home to frighten or punish him or perhaps, more logically, to keep him in his room while she worked that still in the cellar. But she must have had someone to help her with the still, and that person would know that she poured water in front of William's door to keep him in his room.

I looked sharply around the corridor in sudden horror. Of course that person was in the hospital and had already used that knowledge of William twice. But who was it? Could Mr. Thomas, Mrs. Evans, or Ad Miller sneak out of their rooms without being seen? And there was George Moon, Dr. Lawrence, Gavin Bart, Morgue, Linda, and any amount of others.

As I stood there with this new idea beating wildly at my mind William Dana emerged quietly from the solarium at the end of the corridor and walked toward me.

CHAPTER 23

AS WILLIAM DANA approached I realized that I was afraid of him and I knew why. The man was mad. It lay behind his eyes and gleamed through only occasionally, but I felt quite sure of it.

His eyes were blank and dull as he came up to me, and he said mildly,

"It was too hot in my room, Nurse, so I just slipped down to that sun parlor to cool off, but I came right back."

"When did you wake up?" I asked, following him into his room.

"Just a few minutes ago, and it was so hot that I thought, 'The devil with it,' and slipped on down to that sun parlor. But I came right back as soon as I'd cooled off a bit because I know you don't like me to go down there."

I began to feel more sorry for him than afraid of him. He was as docile and repentant as a child, and I said merely, "Well, it's against the rules for you to go down there, you know."

"Yes—yes, I know. But I didn't stay more than a few minutes, you see."

I said, "I see," and let it go. I decided that there was no use trying to explain to him, because he didn't understand, anyway.

He said he thought he might get back to sleep again and immediately turned his face to the wall, with one hand under his cheek, like a tired little boy.

I locked him in. I inserted the key and turned it as quietly as possible, since I did not want to upset him, but as far as I could see through the glass, he never moved at all. I went on down to the solarium to see if he had left or disturbed anything and noticed at once that two of the armchairs had been drawn up to a window, half facing each other, as I had seen them before.

I stood for a long time looking at those two chairs. I supposed that William must have occupied one of them when I had seen them the first time—and now again. I wondered uneasily who on earth his tete-a-tete could be. It seemed hardly possible that it was one of the patients. Certainly William had reached the solarium without my having seen him— probably while I was talking to Mother—but I didn't think that two of them could have managed it. After all, William had been caught on the way back. I decided that he had been telling the truth when he said that he had been in the solarium for only a few minutes, because he had been given a sedative earlier, which would have kept him sleeping for some time.

I headed back for the desk and was caught by Ad Miller standing at his window and making frantic signs.

I sighed and went in to him. "What is it now? Is your bed lumpy? Or do you want the window up or down?"

"Both," said Ad promptly. "I'll just sit in the armchair while you attend to it."

I went over to the window and looked out. Lighted windows in the other buildings glowed through a black pall of heat, and the only result of the afternoon's rain seemed to be an increased humidity.

"When you have finished gazing at the moon," said Ad, "I should like a little of your attention."

I turned away from the window and started to fix up his bed.

"Quite a lot of fun and frolic this morning," he told me, making a wry face. "Game of hide and seek, and these gents were doing the seek. They came pouring in here wearing aprons like a bunch of damned chefs—and no apology for waking me up. They weren't talking, either, although I asked questions steadily. Did they ever find anything?"

I continued to make his bed in silence, and after a moment he laughed. "All right, I'll back up. But you might think this one over. They've had a dick hanging around in the corridor all day—plain clothes, except for his tie—and now that the shades of eve have fallen we are unguarded. For myself, I don't care, because I've lived my life, but it's a dirty trick to play on a young thing like you."

I dropped his pillow, and he handed it to me, smiling faintly into my dismayed face. There should have been a man on guard, and there was not. While Mother was talking to me I had vaguely assumed that he was in the solarium, but I knew now, of course, that that was not so.

I finished Ad's bed in a hurry and started to scrub out, while he complained bitterly about the nurses.

"I'm going to write a hot letter to the board of directors. I'll tell them that they won't even kiss me good night."

"You wouldn't want the board of directors to kiss you good night," I said, busily drying my hands. "There isn't a one of them that's your type."

After I had left Ad I made a hasty search of the wing, found it unguarded, and lost my temper. I went straight to the telephone and had it in my hand when Benny Phipps strolled in, thoughtfully picking his teeth.

I replaced the phone and greeted him with reserve.

He sat down, crossed his legs comfortably, and said, "Hello, girlie, what's cookin'?"

"Where have you been?" I asked coldly.

"Eatin'," said Benny with nonchalance.

"I suppose you know police rules and regulations. I mean I assume it's all right for you to go off and eat while I get murdered up here. It's just," I added earnestly, "that I wouldn't want you to get into any trouble."

Benny's plump face showed signs of a faint distress. "They wouldn't send anythin' up here—only a sandwich," he said defensively. "Anyhow, it's early yet."

"Oh, sure," I said, "it's early. Why don't you go on down to the solarium and catch some sleep and a few germs?"

Benny laughed heartily and all but swallowed his toothpick. "You're a swell kid, and I'd like to take you out some night."

"That would be fun," I said primly, "but what about your wife?"

He became highly indignant and thundered, "I ain't got a wife—I ain't that kind of a heel."

"What kind are you?" I asked politely.

He leaned forward and tapped me on the knee to emphasize his remarks. "Listen, sister, I'm a straight guy—no frills—and I ain't got no fancy line. When I take a girl out I ain't tryin' to make her—I'm courtin' her."

I said it did him credit and that there were very few of his kind left.

He stood up and stretched, looking well pleased with himself. "So how's about steppin' out sometime?"

"I'm the honest kind, myself," I said, "and when people are straightforward with me I'll always be the same way. So I'll have to tell you that unfortunately I'm going steady and I won't be able to go out with you."

A third voice made itself heard at this point and asked interestedly, "With whom are you going steady?"

Benny and I jumped together and turned to find Dr. Lawrence standing behind us.

"Been listenin', fella?" Benny demanded with a hint of menace.

"Certainly not," said Dr. Lawrence. "I'm nothing if not honest and straightforward."

"We're all very fine people, aren't we?" I murmured.

"You better watch out, fella," Benny said, slitting his eyes at the doctor. "You might find yourself gettin' conceited." He stretched again and started off down the corridor. "Guess I'll take a look around."

Dr. Lawrence seated himself. "Would you be kind enough to tell him that my name isn't 'fella'?"

"No," I said and went down to Mrs. Evans' room, because I'd just noticed that her light was on.

Mrs. Evans was distinctly cross. "I've had that light on for ages. What's the matter with you girls, anyway? I'm hot enough to die. What did you do with my fan?"

I murmured an apology and found it for her, and she got several complaints off her chest. "I don't like the atmosphere around here at all. I find, now, that that room next to me is unoccupied, and yet I've heard someone in there several times. And what happened to Mrs. Dana? And another thing, they searched my room this morning, and I can't get anyone to tell me why. What is it all about? I tell you, girl, I will not put up with it much longer."

"I'm sorry," I said firmly, "but I can't talk to you about it. If you're nervous, though, I can lock your door."

"Certainly not," she cried shrilly. "I should feel like a rat in a trap."

"All right," I soothed her. "How's Junior?"

She turned sulky and muttered, "How should I know? Shut up here away from him just when he's at an impressionable age and needs me most. He might even start going out with the girls, and me lying here unable to raise a finger to stop it."

I clicked my tongue in sympathy and hurried out before she could think of anything else.

Dr. Lawrence was still sitting by the desk, and when I came up he said, "Listen, when you said you were going steady did you mean with me?"

"Not by a damn sight," I said promptly.

"Do you mean that? You're not going steady with me and you are going steady with some other fella?"

"Please!" I said. "If you want a quiz turn on the radio."

"Only yesterday," he said thoughtfully, "you and I were as one—and tonight—"

"Tonight," I interrupted, "we face the specters of my steady and Louise Fish."

"Oh," he said. "Oh yes—Louise Fish. Bit of a nuisance, isn't she?"

"Is she? Why don't you behave like our honest Benny and speak more respectfully of your intended?"

He regarded me in silence for a moment and then said uneasily, "I don't like this. I don't like it at all. If you'd get jealous and make a few catty remarks about the Fish I'd feel a lot better."

"All right," I replied agreeably. "I'll say this much—I think Louise has a dismal taste in men."

William Dana's light went on then, so I sped off to answer it.

I unlocked the door quietly and went in to find him sitting up in bed with his hair tousled over his hot, perspiring face.

"Nurse," he said fretfully, "the faucet is dripping over there. I've been hearing it for some time."

I went to the basin and gave both handles a firm twist, although as far as I could see neither was dripping. Without looking at him I asked casually, "Who was sitting with you out in the solarium?"

He replied rather vaguely, "Oh, you mean when I went out there?"

I nodded. "You were sitting and talking with someone, weren't you?"

"Yes," he said quietly. "Yes, it was Aggie."

CHAPTER 24

I GAVE a little gasp and immediately coughed to hide it. When I had composed myself I said sensibly, "No, it wasn't, Mr. Dana. You've been dreaming again."

"It seemed like it was Aggie," he said simply. "I talked to her; I know that. I couldn't see her, but she was there."

"Did you pull up a chair for her to sit on?" I asked.

He nodded. "Yes, I did. I thought maybe—you see, the other time—"

His voice trailed off, and I said quickly, "You sat with her there once before?"

He replied vaguely, "Yes, I guess so."

I scrubbed out and after locking his door went along the corridor with my head in a whirl. William's mind was wandering, and he had killed his sister—I felt convinced of it. And she had left very definite instructions that he was not to have the carpetbag.

I made up my mind to bully Linda into getting it away from him when she came on. After all, she was his niece, and it was more her job than mine.

Dr. Lawrence was still decorating the desk, and I had a sudden conviction that he knew William was mentally infirm and that was why he was hanging around. But didn't he think, too, then, that William had murdered his sister—and if so, why had he not seen to it that he was certified and put away where he could do no further harm?

I sat down at the desk and looked at Dr. Lawrence with new interest. He and Gavin knew about the little hatchet, had been searching for it. It sounded like criminal negligence to me, and I shivered.

He had been watching me and he asked, "What's the matter? Is my back hair coming down?"

I didn't think the spot he was in called for joking, and I said soberly, "You know, don't you, that Mr. Dana is a bit potty?"

His face changed, and a line appeared between his eyebrows. He nodded briefly.

"I suppose it's insubordination to say so," I went on, "but I can't help wondering why you didn't shelve him long ago."

The line disappeared, and he grinned at me. "Overlooking the obvious and rank insubordination, Dana has been in that state for years—vague and slow and rather dull—but to borrow a word from Morgue—and remind me to give it back—definitely not insanic. When I took over the Dana household a few years ago the retiring doctor gave me the dope on both of them—viz., that William's head X-rays plainly showed plush where the brain should have been and that Mrs. Dana enjoyed a serious illness whenever she could find time for it. I have personally confirmed both of these diagnoses, but of course after what has happened—"

The worried line reappeared on his forehead, and I said, "That's why you're around so much, isn't it? To try and find out if he has become insanic?"

"There is no such word as 'insanic,' " observed the voice of Morgue from behind me. "It's time you knew that, Miss Gale. You can never be a good nurse if you are careless in small matters."

I stood up and turned around, and for a moment I was tempted to be guilty of further insubordination, but I controlled myself. "Sorry, Dr. Gill," I said prissily. "I never dreamed the word was not sterling. I picked it up from you."

"That is not amusing, Miss Gale," said Morgue and brushed me aside. "I thought I might find you here, sir," he said to Dr. Lawrence. "I'd like to discuss a very interesting case with you—ran across it the other day."

He sat himself down in my chair and crossed his knees. I believe he had started to put the tips of his fingers together, when Dr. Lawrence said, "Before you start, I'd like to tell you about one of my own cases. Girl by the name of Louise Fish. Sensitive about her last name—neurosis—finally developed scales on her skin. 'Struth."

Morgue's eyes popped, and his mouth fell open

"Tried everything," said Dr. Lawrence, shaking his head, "no success. So now I'm going to marry her. Change the name, you see."

Morgue nodded gravely, his face completely awestruck, and I turned and walked away, conscious of a faint disgust. I did not see how there could be any mistake about the Lawrence-Fish nuptials—Mother usually had her facts straight, and she was no liar—and it seemed rather a mean way to talk about poor Louise. Besides, Dr. Lawrence was on the spot about William Dana and was hanging around only to keep an eye on him.

And in the meantime he was amusing himself with me.

I was in quite a temper by the time I had reached the end of the corridor, and the sight of Benny Phipps, sound asleep in the solarium, with the lights full on and his mouth hanging open, further infuriated me. Benny should have been on the alert, guarding me and my patients, and there he lay. I walked straight over to him, and instead of calling him or shaking his shoulder, I grasped a handful of his hair and tugged.

To my horror the hair came away in my hand, but the next instant I saw that I was holding a toupee. My anger cooled as I regarded this artistic object, but Benny was stirring, and I hastily jammed it back onto his bald head and fled.

Mr. Thomas' light was on, so I took grateful refuge in his room.

Mr. Thomas wanted his door locked. It seemed that he had been uneasy all day after the official search in the morning. "One of them was wearing a police badge of some sort," he told me. "I asked Miss Condit what was going on, but she had quite evidently had instructions not to talk. There have been a lot of people hanging around, and of course I know there's been trouble of some sort. Anyway, I want you to lock my door."

I soothed him rather mechanically and promised to do as he asked, and he seemed to settle down. "I think I'll be able to sleep better with that door locked," he said as I went out.

I locked him in and met Miss Fane and Dr. Bacon doing evening rounds. Duty urged me to tell them what I thought about William Dana's mental condition, but they took it very calmly. Dr. Bacon told me to keep his door locked and not to worry because they were keeping an eye on him.

After they had left I went back to the desk to wait for Linda. Dr. Lawrence and Morgue had disappeared, probably at the approach of Miss Fane and Dr. Bacon, I supposed.

Linda turned up looking as though she had just emerged from a wrapping of tissue paper, and at the same time Benny came pounding up the corridor.

"How's chances for snaffling some eats, girls?" he boomed.

"No telling," Linda murmured, studying her smooth pink nails.

"I'm just going down for supper," I told him. "I'll see if they can send you up a sandwich."

"Thanks, girlie," said Benny. "Like I said before, you're a swell kid."

Linda had glanced up at him, and I noticed now that her eyes were fastened, unwinking, on his head. I stole a look and saw that the smooth part which usually ran down the middle of his head was now running from corner to corner. I fled immediately.

I had a leisurely supper and attended to Benny's sandwich before going off to my room. Once there I removed my shoes, cap, and apron, lighted a cigarette, and then set myself to study Mrs. Dana's framed thoughts, instead of going to sleep, as I should have done.

> *Life is a strange and dangerous thing.*
> *Some people have sons—but I do not.*
> *There is a thrill in all danger. I like to think that perhaps I am dangerous to someone.*
> *Some people have a habit of pulling at their ears—I do not.*
> *It is conceivable that I fear someone.*
> *Some people have removable dental bridges—I don't.*
> *I am not unduly alarmed. I shall protect myself.*
> *Some people are slightly bald. I am not.*

Then came the piece about William and the carpetbag, and that was all.

I watched my cigarette smoke float lazily in the heat of the room and wondered idly if William Dana's insanic condition ran in the family.

And then it hit me. I had been as stupid as Mrs. Dana feared Linda would be. But the thing was quite simple. Mrs. Dana had clearly described her murderer.

CHAPTER 25

SO THIS framed description of a murderer was the "figurative little hatchet" of which Mrs. Dana had spoken. I wondered uncomfortably where the literal one was and why it had not been found. The carpetbag was the obvious place, of course, but I knew that it had been searched dozens of times. I caught my breath in a vexed sound as I realized that I had forgotten to tell Linda to get that carpetbag away from William. I knew that she'd never bother to do it on her own initiative.

My eyes dropped to the framed message again, and I tried to call up a mental image of someone slightly bald pulling at an earlobe, wearing dental bridges, and the proud parent of sons. The result was so unsatisfactory that I jammed the frame impatiently back into the bureau drawer, donned my various pieces of discarded clothing, and took myself out into the hot, sultry night.

I slid around the side of the building and was making for a smooth piece of lawn, when a figure loomed up beside me.

"Let us pretend that you are Louise Fish and take a stroll together," it said, linking arms with me and starting across the grass.

I bit my tongue three times—once rather badly—before I could say airily, "You can pretend I'm Louise, but I'd just as soon be me—sooner, in fact."

"Quite all right," he said agreeably. "But now, to come down to brass tacks, who is this steady of yours?"

"Oh, just a friend," I murmured in some confusion.

"Good!" said Dr. Lawrence. "Just a friend, eh?"

"Well"—I tried to simper a little—"you know—"

He tightened his hold on my arm. "I tell you frankly, I don't like it. I thought I could play both you girls—you and Louise—and now you fling a steady in my face."

"Let's change the subject," I suggested brightly. "For instance, when did you last visit your dentist?"

"Dentist?" he repeated, surprised. "I dunno. The pest gets after me every six months. How about you?"

"I'll have to go soon—maybe I'll need to have some out. Have you had any out?"

"Three," he said absently. "About this steady of yours, I don't seem to have noticed him around the hospital."

"He can't get in. What do you do about the gaps?"

"What gaps?"

"The gaps where your teeth used to be."

"Oh—nothing. The dentist warned me that my face would fall in, and that intrigued me to such an extent that I refused a bridge and I am now awaiting results."

I tried to look at him, but it was too dark to see any expression on his face, and I was left with a feeling of doubt about the bridges. But I remembered Benny's policy of leaving no stone unturned, so I plowed on.

"How's your son?" I asked next.

"My son?" He tried to look at me then and probably was not any more successful than I had been. "To tell you the truth," he said after a moment, "Louise prefers that we make no mention of him until after the wedding."

I felt completely exasperated and told him, rather shortly, that I'd have to be getting in.

We veered away from the lawn and headed toward the hospital, and he observed mildly, "I'd really like to know who your steady is."

"What good would it do you to know?" I asked, getting off a laugh that cracked slightly in the upper register.

"I should call on him with my checkbook and buy him off."

"So you're rich?"

"Rolling in it. That's why the Fish clan trapped me."

I said, "Listen, a joke's a joke, but you go too far."

He left me at the elevator, and I went on up to find Linda looking scared and reproachful.

"Didn't you get them to send a sandwich up for that man? He's gone off to forage for food."

"Certainly I arranged for his sandwich. But a sandwich is only an hors d'oeuvre to Benny Phipps. Do you mean you're all alone?"

She nodded. "I'm simply frightened to death too."

"Say, Linda," I said suddenly. "You ought to get that carpetbag away from your uncle; there must be something in it that he's not supposed to have. You could sneak in and take it."

"Oh, let him have his old carpetbag," she said crossly. "Aunt Aggie can't boss me any more the way she was always trying to." She shrugged the problem away from her, and her face changed to an expression of happy intimacy. "Norma, I have something to tell you, but it's a secret. Cross your heart and hope to die you won't tell anyone."

I gave the promise, knowing full well that whatever the tidings, Linda herself would promptly spread them far and wide.

She came closer and whispered dramatically into my ear, "My dear, I'm engaged!"

"No!" I exclaimed. "For heaven's sake! Who?"

"Ad Miller," she breathed excitedly.

My knees gave way, and I sank onto a chair, utterly stunned. I knew that it would be easier to trap an ermine than to trap Ad Miller, and Linda did not even have any money! Unless her aunt had left her some.

"Congratulations!" I murmured dazedly. "How—how did you pull it off?"

"Norma!" I think she actually stamped her foot. "Ad and I love each other, and the engagement very naturally followed."

"Naturally," I said, beginning to recover a little. "I'm all thrilled, Linda—I think it's grand. When is it going to be?"

"Oh, sometime soon. My dear, I'm so excited I don't know what I'm doing. We'll live in Ad's apartment, and I'll keep on nursing until he gets a decent position."

I approved of that and said so. "Once you graduate you'll always have a living, and that's a good thing to have tucked under your belt. Although I suppose your aunt left you something."

"My aunt!" Linda yipped scornfully. "She wouldn't leave me anything—she always said she wouldn't—only that old piano in the living room, and I know it wouldn't suit Ad's furniture—I know that from instinct. Aunt Aggie said she'd leave her money in trust for Uncle William, and Gavin was the trustee—or whatever you call it—and then I think Gavin gets the money when Uncle William dies. She had it all arranged, you see. Gavin is supposed to live with Uncle William and take care of him, and I was supposed to live there, too, and do the housework. I told her that part of it was out and I guess that put me out of the money—if I was ever in it."

"She had it all laid out in a pattern, didn't she?" I said thoughtfully. "Did she leave a will?"

"Oh, I guess so," Linda said carelessly.

"But don't you know? Haven't you heard anything about it?"

She shook her head. "Gavin is seeing to all that sort of stuff. Listen— I can't stand here all night. I'll see you later."

She went off, and I shook my head and said, "Tch, tch," and felt like Mother.

Ad Miller's light went on; and when I got to his room I seemed to be looking at him with new eyes.

"Did you want me to scratch your back?" I asked.

"No," said Ad, and his voice sounded feeble, "I want sympathy."

"Why?"

"You know very well why," he said indignantly. "You know as well as I do that that girl got herself engaged to me in as neat a way as I've ever seen it done. Me. Addison Miller. What a crashing comedown."

It was too much for me. I sat down on the straight chair and laughed until my breath was gone, and I began to think I'd strangle.

In the end Ad brought me his glass of water and offered it to me anxiously. The gesture brought me around, and I stopped laughing and stood up.

"Mr. Miller," I said, wiping my eyes, "I have no intention of drinking out of your germ-ridden tumbler. Please put it back where you got it and get into bed."

He climbed back into bed without a word and sat there looking digni-fied and offended.

"I can't seem to rake up any sympathy for you," I said severely. "Linda is a sweet, attractive girl, and you're a heel to talk like that, anyway."

"Right," he said, "I am a heel. And why would she want to marry me? Anyone ought to know I'd make a lousy husband. I wonder—does she seem to be pleased about the whole thing?"

"Delighted," I said firmly. "Don't be so discouraged; you might turn out to be the best husband in seven counties."

"Boy!" said Ad, staring into space. "They'd be some seven coun-ties."

He protested vociferously as I left, and "I want to talk over my trous-seau with you," was the last thing I heard.

I closed the door with my elbow in the approved manner and then stood and stared at the inevitable and frightening pool of water in front of William Dana's door.

CHAPTER 26

I GLANCED up and down the dim, quiet corridor and tried to quell my sharply rising fear by trying to figure out exactly when that water could have been spilled. I thought at first it might have been done when I was in Ad's room and realized almost at once that that was impossible. I had only to raise my head and glance through Ad's window to have seen anyone in front of William's door. Too much risk, if the person who was doing it wanted to remain anonymous.

I went back to the desk and sat down, leaving the splash of water to be exhibited to Kenny when he returned. And I determined to insist that the Shaw man should be told about it too.

I made another effort to fit someone to Mrs. Dana's description and started off with slightly bald heads. I ran into difficulty at once, because "slightly bald" was a vague term, and Mrs. Dana's conception might eas-ily have differed from mine. As a matter of fact, you could have called Mrs. Evans slightly bald. She hid it well, and it was not very noticeable, but she had a decidedly thin spot on the top of her head.

Gavin's hair was receding at the temples, or else it grew unusually far back. Dr. Lawrence seemed to have plenty; George Moon and William Dana were slightly bald, and Mr. Thomas was a little more than slightly.

Linda and Betty Condit had luxuriant heads of hair, and Morgue had entirely too much. It grew so far down on his forehead that when he frowned his hair and eyebrows were as one. Ad Miller's hair was adequate but obviously receding.

I stood up restlessly and, after a moment's indecision, moved my chair around so that its back was against the wall. I sat down and immediately found myself looking at the splash of water and had to drag my eyes away.

There was no sound from the elevator of Benny's return, and I spared him a few curses before forcing my mind to consider the murderer's habit of pulling at an earlobe. Speculation was a complete washout, though, because I simply could not remember having seen anyone pulling at an earlobe recently.

I proceeded to the matter of sons and conversely had too much material on my hands. Mrs. Evans and Mr. Thomas not only admitted it but bragged of it. Ad Miller apparently had no legal sons, and yet it was possible that somewhere in his shady past he had married and begotten, and the same thing applied to Dr. Lawrence, Gavin, George Moon—and even Betty Condit. I felt quite sure that Linda had no son, or she would certainly have, told me about it in the strictest confidence.

There was no data on the removable bridge situation, with the exception of Dr. Lawrence's three gaps. And for all I knew, he might have had bridges for his gaps and buried them in the back yard to throw me off the scent.

I was dizzy by that time, so I gave it up for the moment; perhaps I'd give it up altogether, I reflected tiredly. I'd hand the framed description over to Millard Shaw and wash my hands of it.

Benny came back at that point, and I asked him coldly if he'd had a good meal. He said tolerantly that it would do, and at the same time I noticed with guilty relief that his part was now straight again.

"Are you allowed to leave the floor while you eat?" I asked, for the sake of saying something that would keep my mind and eyes away from his hair.

"Sure," said Benny. "I didn't leave the hospital, see?"

"How is the case going?"

"Lousy," said Benny simply. "Dead ends."

"I heard that Mrs. Dana ran a still," I said tentatively.

"Where'dja hear that?"

"Linda was down at the house and saw it."

Benny said, "Hmm, it ain't been run in years, but I'd give a lot to know who used to take the stuff off her. We can't get no leads on that."

"Oh, but you will," I murmured.

"Sure, I guess so." He began to warm up. "'Sfunny —that old dame livin' in that dump, doin' her own work, and with dough all the time."

"Who gets it now?"

"The girl gets a bit, the nephew more, and the old man a nice little income for life."

So Linda inherited, after all, and she had never expected it. I felt a surge of pleasurable excitement. She could get some nice clothes for the wedding! I firmly put aside a nasty, nagging little consideration as to whether Ad knew of the legacy and turned my mind to other things.

"That pool of water is in front of Mr. Dana's door again," I told Benny. "It seems to be there most of the time now."

Benny put on a detecting sort of expression and went down to examine it, and I went along with him. He frowned down at the splash for a while and then raised his head and studied the ceiling immediately above.

"I hate to disappoint you," I said, "but the roof doesn't leak."

"Well, you gotta consider everythin', and it seems such a dopey thing for anyone to do. I'd say somebody around here had forgot he was a gentleman—except I never knew anyone in my life could spit that big. Are you sure you girls ain't spillin' somethin'?"

I shook my head. "If we spill anything we wipe it up immediately— or else."

He stood for a while in silence, looking gloomily down at the water and munching on his toothpick.

"Hadn't you better get hold of Shaw?" I suggested. "I think he should know about it, and there's something I want to tell him, anyway."

Benny raised his eyes and gave me what he probably thought was a piercing look. "You can tell me anything you got on your mind, girlie. That's what I'm here for."

But I didn't want to tell him, for some reason, and I said uncomfortably, "Oh, it's nothing much, really. I'd just like to see him."

"You're seem' me," Benny persisted. "I'm his representative, and anythin' you got on your mind you better tell me. Delay may be dangerous—you oughta know that."

I shook my head and walked back to the desk, and after a moment Benny pounded past me and went out to the elevator, offended dignity showing in every line of him. I supposed he had gone off to contact Shaw, and I was bitterly sorry that I had brought the thing up; it was so frightening to be alone.

Action was better than sitting and thinking, and I made up my mind to get the carpetbag away from William without further delay.

I was a little startled to find his room unlocked and then realized that Linda must be responsible. William was awake and raised his head as I came in.

"What is it, Nurse?"

I made his bed more comfortable and turned him over so that he was facing the wall. "Now I want you to close your eyes and lie perfectly still for at leas ten minutes," I said quietly. "Don't move and don't pay any attention to me, and I think you may be able to get off to sleep. You need sleep, you know."

He murmured something about not wanting to sleep, anyway, but did as he was told, and I went straight for the carpetbag, determined to remove it once and for all.

I realized, as I walked out with it, that it was extraordinarily heavy, much heavier than a bundle of papers and a bit of carpet should have been, and I was reminded of the time I had carried it to Mrs. Dana, when the same thing had occurred to me.

Out in the hall a conviction that the bag contained a hatchet—gruesome and bloodstained—forced me to set it down while I recovered my breath. I was hot and damp and shivering a little at the same time, but I had made up my mind to find that hatchet if it were in the bag to find.

I picked the thing up again and stumbled across to the vacant room next to Mrs. Evans, where I dropped it onto the floor. I released the catch with shaking fingers and had started to feel carefully along the lining, when a voice behind me brought my heart thudding into my throat.

I flung around to find Dr. Lawrence looking at me; his face livid with fury. He said, "Close that bag and get out of here at once."

CHAPTER 27

I STRAIGHTENED my back and faced him squarely. "What do you mean?" I asked.

"What I say," he replied coldly. "Get out of here and leave that bag alone."

Anger stirred in me and tingled into my finger tips. I began, "By what authority—" and got no farther. He laid a firm hand on my arm, snapped off the light, pushed me out into the corridor and closed the door behind us.

He released my arm and said curtly, "Now go on back to your desk and get on with your own work——and leave the police to do theirs. Undoubtedly you could show them a thing or two, but after all, they have their own marks to make in the world and the mouths of their kiddies to feed, and you wouldn't want to do them out of their jobs."

There were several things I could have said, but to my fury and self-contempt two hot angry tears burned in my eyes, and I turned away just before they dripped over. I walked slowly back to the desk, surreptitiously mopping up as I went. I sat down in what I hoped was a properly casual manner, and after a moment I glanced carelessly down the corridor.

Dr. Lawrence was still standing outside the door of the vacant room. He was smoking a cigarette and appeared to be staring up at me. I hunched my shoulders over the desk and got to work—or pretended to.

But double interruption showed up in the persons of Millard Shaw and Benny. Shaw nodded to me, and then his eye fell on Dr. Lawrence, and his brows shot up. The doctor advanced slowly to the desk, greeted Shaw coolly and Benny not at all.

"What's the matter?" Shaw barked.

"Nothing," said Dr. Lawrence sourly.

"Standing guard down there?"

Dr. Lawrence showed a faint hesitation and then said, "No. Just thinking."

Shaw abandoned him and turned to me. "What have you to tell me?"

I told him of the trip Linda and I had taken out to the house and about the framed note, and instead of being grateful, he bristled with irritation.

"How did you come to get in? I have a man out there."

I modestly described the procedure that had outwitted the guardian of Mrs. Dana's house, and instead of giving me applause Shaw interrupted irritably. "But the side door was locked."

"So it was," I agreed, beginning to get annoyed myself. "A cheap old lock with an invitation hanging out to any old key. If you'd wanted to keep people out of that door I should have thought you'd have nailed it, at least."

"Never mind the advice," Shaw snapped. "We'll get along without it."

I said, "Oh yes, eventually, I suppose," and received a warning nudge from Benny which felt as though it had left a dent in me. It shut me up, though, and I was conscious of a dim gratitude for Benny. He seemed to have my welfare at heart, and guilty remorse faintly shadowed my mind when I remembered that I had not only pulled his hair off but replaced it improperly for all to see.

Shaw asked, "What else did you take from the house? "

"Jam," I said shortly.

"Jam!"

"We thought it might be nice," I explained confusedly.

Shaw was silent for a moment, his sharp gray eyes thoughtful.

He demanded presently, "Where is it now?"

"I think we left it on the floor of the bus," I said meekly and was considerably startled by the verbal explosion that followed. However, when the debris was finally cleared away it emerged that Shaw had been referring to the framed note and I to the jam.

I hastily located the note in my bureau drawer, and Shaw turned on Benny and abruptly directed him to get it at once.

Benny showed signs of acute discomfort and actually blushed. He muttered, "I—er—don't think men are allowed in there."

Shaw turned on him and asked viciously, "How could that affect you in any way? Go on over and get it at once."

I hated to add to Benny's discomfort, but I felt obliged to specify, "It's sort of wrapped up in a pink satin brassiere," and he went off with the back of his neck glowing bright red.

Shaw turned on me then and put me through a searching and exhaustive questionnaire. We went all over the splashes of water outside William's door, but I said nothing of my latest contact with the carpetbag, because Dr. Lawrence was sitting beside us, listening to the whole thing, and I was not going to admit that he had run me out of that room like a naughty child. I did stop Shaw and asked him if we could have more privacy, but he said impatiently that it didn't matter, and Dr. Lawrence continued to flap his ears.

Benny returned eventually, wearing a relieved smile, and clutching the picture frame in his hands. He had so far recovered his equanimity as to study the thing over Shaw's shoulder.

I decided to have my coffee and went off into the diet kitchen feeling glad to get away from them.

Dr. Lawrence wandered in after me, still smoking, and I said coldly, "Be careful where you put the butt. If it's found around here I'll get into trouble."

"You are in trouble," he replied briefly.

My eyes opened very wide, and I asked, "What on earth do you mean? What trouble am I in?"

"I am not in the dark," he replied significantly, "about why you were nosing into that bag."

"Well, all right, and why does that mean I'm in trouble? Or that you should treat me as though I had just kicked my poor old mother?"

He disposed of his cigarette without bothering to reply, and I turned my attention to the coffee. When it was ready I asked him if he'd have some, and he nodded absently.

We drank coffee in a silence that seemed to droop gloomily over the entire kitchen. When I had finished I put my cup down with a bang, and stood up.

"Listen," I said angrily, "if you have a mad on I wish you'd go and have it somewhere else—maybe the Fish woman would like to coax you out of it. But as far as I'm concerned, I'd rather not see your ugly face any more tonight."

He put his cup down on the sink and moved over to me with very little change in his expression. Without preliminary he enfolded me in his arms and kissed me as expertly as Ad Miller could have done. He looked down at me for a moment then and said, "Now keep your mouth shut. Don't say anything, no matter what happens."

He took himself off, and I started to follow, intending to ask him what he meant, but my training got the better of me and I washed the cups first.

When I returned to the desk I found that Shaw and Benny had disappeared and I saw Dr. Lawrence heading for the vacant room in which we had left the carpetbag.

I did not see why I should be excluded from an investigation of that bag when I had gone to the trouble of getting it away from William, and I walked straight down the corridor and followed Dr. Lawrence into the room.

The bag was open, and he was crouched over it with his hands inside. He seemed to be pulling at the bottom, and as I looked the entire floor of the bag came away, revealing a hidden space beneath, which had a depth of about two inches. My rising excitement died quickly, however, for the space was empty.

Dr. Lawrence looked at it for a moment and then rose to his feet. "It's not there," he said, and his voice sounded curiously heavy.

"What did you think was going to be there?" I asked.

He turned on me almost savagely. "Don't be a fool!" And after a moment, "What did you do with it?"

I backed away and refrained from slapping his face only because I considered it too old-fashioned.

"If you mean what I think you do," I said thickly, "you can go and boil your head, because I don't want to see it again—or any part of you."

"She kept the damned little hatchet in that space, of course," he said, ignoring me, "and someone knew of it and used it on her."

"Of course," I agreed. "And you seemed to know about that false bottom, which is interesting when you come to think about it, isn't it?"

He took no notice of me and muttered, "Can't understand the police—they should have found it."

I could have enlightened him on that point, but I didn't bother. Since the bag had been transferred to William's room they had probably supposed it belonged to him and had searched it only cursorily.

Dr. Lawrence turned abruptly and said, "I'm going to get Shaw back here. If he's not downstairs I'll phone."

He went off, and I closed the door of the vacant room and stood uncertainly in the corridor with a new foreboding sort of fear closing around me. I hated Shaw, Benny, and Dr. Lawrence indiscriminately for leaving me alone in that silent, ominous wing.

I moved a little and looked for the splash of water outside William's door, but it had been wiped up. I wondered vaguely who had done it and supposed that it was Benny under Shaw's direction.

As I looked I noticed something small and black lying on the floor a little farther down the corridor, and I walked forward to investigate.

The thing was William Dana's black thumb guard.

And the thumb seemed to be inside it.

CHAPTER 28

I INSTINCTIVELY moved back, feeling for the support of the solid wall behind my shoulders. I was battered by a crashing wave of horror, and yet I was conscious of a little thread of clear thought running through the confusion. I should have gone away with Mother—it would have been better to have followed her strong common sense than my own rather misty idea of noble duty.

Duty. My mind cleared, and I pulled myself away from the wall. I was alone in the wing and had the responsibility of four patients, even though they were a crummy lot. I choked back a hysterical desire to laugh and made myself look at the horrid little object on the floor. I noticed, now, that there was no sign of blood around the thing, and my fear and excitement steadied to the point that I was able to creep forward and pick it up.

It was a false thumb—a rather clumsy affair covered with the black leather thumb guard. I turned it over, handling it with distaste, and remembered how poor William had snarled at my offers to see to his damaged thumb. He was sensitive about it, apparently, and did not want anyone to know.

But how did it come to be out in the corridor? I glanced up and down, trying desperately to ignore a surge of terror that seemed to start somewhere in the pit of my stomach. The carpetbag—it had been heavy when I carried it into the vacant room, heavy with a small hatchet which had subsequently disappeared from the space beneath the false bottom. Someone had taken that hatchet—someone who knew where to look for it.

I drew a quick, sharp breath, whirled around, and went straight to William Dana's room. He was not there, of course; I hadn't really expected to find him. The door was unlocked, and I tried frantically to remember about it. Linda had left it open when she had gone off—at least I had found it open and I supposed she had been into the room for something and had forgotten to lock up after her. And I must have forgotten it too.

I abandoned speculation and ran for the phone, only to be given the bad news that Millard Shaw and Benny Phipps had departed for an unknown destination. A cool voice assured me that every effort would be used to get in touch with him and then offered me George Moon to bridge the gap.

I hung up with tears of pure fury in my eyes. I did not want George; I wanted Shaw and Benny and a detachment of patrolmen.

I stood by the desk for a while, and then I realized that I was still clutching the thumb in its black guard, and I walked slowly down to . William's room and put it on his bureau. Out in the corridor again I hesitated and looked fearfully down toward the solarium. I had a queer, certain conviction that William Dana was down there, but I simply could not force myself to go and look.

Instead I returned to the desk to wait for George. I waited and waited, with the silence singing in my ears, and at last I telephoned again. There was a faint hint of impatience in the cool voice this time, and it informed me that George had had his instructions and should be with me any minute.

I could not sit there waiting any longer, so I went into the diet kitchen and poured myself some milk. I drank it fast, trying all the time to ignore the voice of my conscience which insisted that I should be at the desk watching for someone carrying a small bloodstained hatchet.

I cleaned the glass with a sense of rising panic and was just putting it away when I heard a noise.

It was not loud and not identifiable—just a vague sound that nevertheless started my heart thudding uncomfortably. I remember whispering, "It's not a hospital noise; I know all the hospital noises," and then telling myself not to be a fool.

I crept out to the desk and looked down the corridor and thought that something moved.

But the corridor was empty, and I straightened my shoulders and tried to be sensible. "A noise and a movement," I thought, "and yet you don't really hear the one or see the other. It's just nerves."

George had not appeared, and I felt sure, by now, that he was not coming. As a matter of fact, I could quite well imagine him putting on his hat and simply walking out when he received instructions to go to my wing and search for a man!

I tried to laugh at that and found I couldn't, and the next thing I knew I was walking purposefully down the corridor with the intention of looking in on the patients and making sure that they were all right.

I was able to satisfy myself about Mrs. Evans without even waking her up, although I was not particularly quiet. I went into Ad Miller's room and found him snoring loudly, which exasperated me to a point where I could have slapped his face. I needed a little company—someone to talk to—and the first time I could have used Ad I found him flat on his back and dead to the world. I thought of getting even by telling Linda that he snored and realized wearily that Linda was in the bemused state where Ad's snores might even be attractive.

Mr. Thomas was snoring, too, though more gently. I did not bother to clear my throat or anything of that sort; I let him sleep on and went out quietly.

In the corridor I stood looking down at the solarium. It was closer now, and the chances were that William Dana was sitting quietly in a chair by one of the windows, trying to cool off. In fact, he might have gone to sleep—probably had. And he could easily have dropped the thumb on his way down.

That last sounded a bit weak, since I knew he was sensitive about the thumb and would almost certainly be aware of having dropped it. However, I put the thought away from me and started bravely toward the solarium, humming as I went, to make it seem more natural.

The humming began to quaver when I reached the wide dark arch that led into the place, but I stepped firmly inside and switched on the light.

For a while I floated in darkness, and then I became conscious of a misty perplexity because the solarium was only dimly lighted. I struggled with this for a while and then dragged my eyes open and tried to move. Pain shot through my head, and now the solarium seemed garish with a light too strong for human eyes. My mind moved sluggishly against the problem of how I came to be sitting on the floor, leaning against a chair, and then with a tremendous effort I managed to get my eyes open again.

Somebody was sitting on the floor quite close to me, leaning against the wall, but his face was veiled in blood, so that I could see only a part of the mouth grinning at me.

CHAPTER 29

I BEGAN a desperate struggle against failing consciousness to get away from the dead, grinning figure that was propped up against the wall. The eyes stared through a mask of blood with the blank opacity of a doll, and yet they seemed to follow me.

My head began to spin around, and I had a vague feeling that it was attached to my neck by one single frail thread. Someone was trying to scream, and someone was giving feeble little whimpers, and I was both of them. I crawled along the floor, taking exaggerated care of that thin thread that held my head to my shoulders, and then I clutched at the chair beside me and tried to raise myself. But the dizziness became much worse, and I fell back and watched the ceiling lights going off like rockets.

Into the growing dusk of my faculties a muttered curse suddenly injected itself, and my eyes opened almost without effort. Dr. Lawrence's face was close above my own; and I could feel his arms, under my body, tense for a moment as he lifted me. As long as he carried me I was content, but when I felt myself being lowered to a bed I stretched out my hand and said, "No."

He took hold of my hand and I managed to open my eyes.

"What is it?" he asked. "What do you mean, 'no'?"

"Don't leave me alone. Don't go away and leave me—"

"I must telephone," he said. "I'll come back at once. You know this room—it's right beside the desk. I'll be just outside. Don't be a sissy, anyway—it's only a conk on the head."

I whispered, "All right, but come back again right away," and he nodded and went quickly out of the room.

I began to feel better. The buzzing in my head was fainter and, lying flat like that, I hardly felt the dizziness. I ran a careful exploratory hand over my head and found a bump—a big one—and it seemed to be a bit sticky. I drew a long breath and thought idiotically, "At least it's in a place where I can hide it with my hair—if I live, that is."

I remembered the lolling dummy in the solarium, then, and was lost again in a whirling vertigo.

I opened my eyes after a while and found that Dr. Lawrence was standing at the foot of the bed looking down at me. "Feel better?" he asked.

"Yes," I said shortly.

He moved around to the side of the bed and, leaning over, very gently examined the bump on my head. He straightened up after a moment and said, "I'm not going to touch it—let the boys see for themselves. There's no doubt that somebody beaned you; you could hardly have got a crack like that by falling against anything in the solarium."

"I'm glad to have it proved," I said, trying not to lose my temper. "I suppose you would not have taken my word for it."

He sat down on the side of the bed. "As it happens, I would have taken your word for it, but I'm glad that goose egg is such a honey. They'll probably get Morgue out of his comfortable little bed, and he'll have to admit that someone tried to brain you. I expect Morgue will be delegated to patch you up, too, but don't be too alarmed about it—he knows a little first aid, our Morgue."

"You listen to me, James Lawrence," I said clearly. "If I had decided to commit a murder I'd certainly make sure that I didn't stumble and fall when I had it done."

He laughed a little and pulled out his cigarette case. "Before the mob comes pouring up here tell me one thing. Why did you have the bag in that vacant room? And why were you searching it?"

But I was still angry that he could have suspected me of any complicity in Mrs. Dana's murder.

"I was looking for a little ax so that I could kill somebody," I said nastily.

He stood up quickly and said, "Shh," and the next instant the room seemed to be filled with people.

I closed my eyes so that I would not have to look at them, and after a while I heard Dr. Lawrence say, "Down here," and they all piled out again.

I opened one eye cautiously and saw that Linda had been left with me.

"Oh, you poor thing!" she exclaimed. "What in the world ever happened?"

I shook my head, conscious, all of a sudden, that I was desperately tired. "I don't know—only there's another one down there in the solarium. Murdered."

She screamed prettily and cried, "Oh, Norma, who? Tell me!"

I started to say, "I'm not certain—" but she ran out of the room without waiting to listen.

She was back again so promptly that I was sure she had been told to stay with me and reprimanded for not doing it. She appeared to be relieved about something and explained it by saying simply, "I was afraid it was Ad."

"Then who is, it?" I asked feverishly. "For God's sake, tell me."

Her face clouded, and two tears glittered in her eyes. "It's Uncle William," she wailed and began to cry.

I had been hoping desperately that it wouldn't be William Dana—I had marked him for the insane murderer—and then everything would have been cleared up. I gritted my teeth and said to Linda, "Hadn't you better get in touch with your cousin?"

She mopped at her eyes, nodded, and went out into the hall. I heard her fussing around with the phone, and presently she came back. "He's not there, as usual," she said bitterly. "He's always had fun while Aunt Aggie gave him money, and she never gave me a dime. All I ever got was a handkerchief or a glove box at Christmas, and she made those herself."

I was tempted to tell her about her inheritance, but a consideration that Benny might have been wrong about it stopped me, since I did not want her to be disappointed.

"Uncle William was always nice to me, though," she said and broke into a storm of sobs that began to look like hysterics.

I watched her uneasily, wishing that some of the others would come back, but she presently pulled herself together and had nearly dried off when Millard Shaw marched into the room.

Dr. Lawrence came in, too, and I began to wonder if he had been made a deputy sheriff or something. They ranged themselves around the bed, and Shaw said briskly, "Now, Miss Gale, I want your statement."

Statement! I closed my eyes and moaned, "O God! Somebody get me a lawyer."

Dr. Lawrence cleared his throat loudly and, it seemed to me, unnecessarily, and my eyes flew to his face in terror. However, he seemed to be merely amused. He was wearing one of those faint superior smiles that doctors always assume when they want to tell you not to be an ass. He said, "Tell the inspector what happened, Norma—that's all."

I relaxed a little and told my tale, but all the way through I kept worrying about the carpetbag. I wondered where it was and whether that space under the false bottom was still empty or not, but I managed to finish my story without having referred to it.

Shaw brought it up immediately. "About that carpetbag—I suppose you took it across the hall to the vacant room."

I snatched a quick glance at Dr. Lawrence and saw him light a cigarette and throw the match onto the floor. He was frowning.

I swallowed and said, "Yes."

"Why?" asked Shaw.

"That note of Mrs. Dana's," I said faintly. "She said her brother was not to have it."

Shaw nodded. "The bag belonged to Mrs. Dana, though. How did he get hold of it?"

Linda moved out of the shadows by the door and said, "I gave it to him. He asked for it."

Shaw stirred and shifted his eyes to her face. "I see. But you were told to keep that door locked and not to touch anything in the room."

Linda showed fight. "I know, but that old bag was as much his as hers—he had a right to it—and when he asked for it I just went right along and got it for him."

"Did he say why he wanted it?" Shaw asked quietly.

"He said there was something in it he might need, and he'd like to have it since Aggie couldn't use it any more."

Shaw took a turn about the room and then, ignoring Linda, who still had her chin up at him, asked me what I'd done with the bag once I had it in the vacant room.

I started to tell him, but Dr. Lawrence interrupted almost at once and told the whole thing himself. He left out the harsh words he and I had had and made a dull, factual story out of what was left.

Shaw received it in silence and took another turn about the room while he digested it, and then he stepped to the door and called Morgue.

Morgue came in eagerly and was briefly requested to examine my head. He leaped joyfully to the task and went over the entire area with care and gravity, not overlooking a scar I had acquired at the age of three. He gave over, at last, and prepared to deliver his findings to Shaw.

He straightened up first, slightly bent his head, drew his brows down, and cleared his throat.

"Gentlemen."

"I'm here too," Dr. Lawrence murmured.

Morgue gave him a puzzled look, and Shaw said impatiently, "All right, Dr. Gill, let's get on with it."

Morgue got on with it. He spoke of a contusion, wandered off onto a branch line in which he pointed out the possibilities of concussion and fracture, recommended X-ray to set all minds at rest on these two formidable points, and then gave it as his modest opinion that it would turn out to be nothing but a goose egg which would deflate in its own good time. Only he didn't say "goose egg." He ended up by observing that there was some blood around the contusion, although the skin was unbroken

CHAPTER 30

I WAILED, "Oh, Linda, wash it off," and could not think of anything else until she had made my head clean again.

As soon as she had finished and I was able to relax a little I chewed over what Morgue had said and decided with a certain amount of annoyance that he had made light of my injury. Yet Dr. Lawrence had declared that I could not have done it by falling against anything and seemed confident that Morgue would back him up. I wanted to ask Dr. Lawrence about it and raised my head to look for him, but he was standing just outside the door and seemed to be deep in a grave and earnest argument with Shaw and Morgue.

I dropped my head back onto the pillow and hoped piously that my position was being properly defended.

Linda had put away the soap and bowl of water which she had used in cleaning my hair, and she now perched herself on the end of my bed and began to cry quietly into her handkerchief. Once she whispered, "I feel much worse than I did about Aunt Aggie."

I tried to say something comforting, but she continued to cry for some time. And then quite suddenly the storm was over. She straightened her shoulders, blew her nose, and made up her face. But that was always the way with Linda—either she was in the depths of despair or she was on top of the world; there seemed to be very little middle course.

I caught a glimpse of a group of men in the corridor and heard them go pounding down to the solarium. Linda got off the bed immediately and went and stuck her head out the door.

"They're going to take pictures," she announced after a while.

"Pictures!" I repeated, astounded.

She came back to the bed. "Of course—they always do. I don't remember why, exactly, except I think they make a collection of them and hang them in a museum they have—but only the big pots are allowed to go in and look."

I closed my eyes and murmured, "Please don't be an idiot."

She dropped onto the end of the bed and said, "Poor Uncle William—he was an old dear. You know, he wasn't half so—so mutilated as Aunt Aggie. He'd bled a lot, and that made him look kind of ghastly, but he hadn't been—well—savaged, like Aunt Aggie."

"Did they find the weapon?" I asked.

"Weapon?" A look of alert interest came into her face. "I don't know. I'll go and find out."

She went off and was back shortly, burgeoning with news. "They found it!" she told me in a shrill whisper. "In that old carpetbag—it has a false bottom. I never knew there was a false bottom in the thing."

"It was put back there after I was hit," I said thoughtfully.

Linda gave a hysterical little giggle. "That Benny Phipps—was he getting it! The inspector told him he should have suspected a false bottom when he searched the bag. And he told him a lot of other things too. Benny's ears were lobster-red, and he looked fit to have a stroke."

"Poor Benny," I said. "I don't know what his official title is, but I'll always think of it as 'the goat.'"

"Oh, don't waste your sympathy. Benny's doing all right. If they didn't bawl him out all the time, his head would get too big for his hat. Anyway, he's made up with his girlfriend, and they've even set the date for the wedding. He promised always to wear a tie if they had company, but he said he couldn't promise about his coat because sometimes it's too hot for a coat. So she gave in on that point, provided he'd remove his sleeve garters along with the coat."

"I shall be more than happy to listen to Benny's private life at some other time," I said courteously. "Right now if you don't tell me what's going on out there I'll blow a fuse."

"Oh well," she sighed, "I don't know so much myself. I heard them say if you *were* hit on the head by somebody he must have come up behind you, because the bump is at the back. Inspector Shaw had to shut them up."

"Shut who up?" I asked querulously.

"Why, Morgue and that conceited Lawrence man. They kept arguing whether you could have got that bump by falling or not. Morgue was having a wonderful time; he called that bump on your dome a bruise, a contusion, and an ecchymosis at various times, according to how he felt about it at the moment, I guess."

"They're crazy," I said bitterly. "I'm supposed to have killed poor William, tripped and fallen when the job was done, and then returned the weapon to the carpetbag before I lost consciousness. What kind of a weapon was it?"

She said, "What's that?" vaguely, and then, "Don't be silly, Norma. Of course they don't think anything of the sort."

"The weapon, Linda?" I said impatiently.

"Oh, it was a little ax or hatchet or whatever you call it—you know the sort of thing. Washington's Birthday. Well, anyway, it was only a little one, but good and sharp. I guess somebody had it sharpened. The head was bloodstained—plenty—but the handle had been washed off in the basin in that vacant room where the carpetbag was."

I closed my eyes and thought it over. I had been knocked out because someone needed time to wash the prints from the handle of that ax and return it to the bag. William had been killed after Shaw and Benny had left and while Dr. Lawrence and I were having coffee in the diet kitchen. Someone must have been desperate to get William out of the way, for the time had been perilously short. As it was, the doctor and I had come out of the kitchen too soon, and of course when we looked in the bag the ax was not there. William was already dead at that time, his artificial thumb lying on the floor and his killer hiding and waiting for a chance to return the ax to the carpetbag. But I had been in the way and had brought matters to a climax at last by going down to the solarium. The hue and cry attendant upon the discovery of the murder had to be delayed until the ax was washed and returned to its place, and so I was dealt with.

I had been hit from behind, of course; it could not be any other way, because I had actually stood out side the entrance to the solarium and stretched my hand around to turn on the lights, so that I must have seen anyone who was not directly behind me. I remembered that I had hummed a tune to keep my courage up and supposed that that was why I had not heard whoever was behind me. I raised my hand and gingerly felt my head. There was no doubt that the bruise, contusion, or ecchymosis was well toward the back.

I heard Miss Fane's voice and opened my eyes.

"Linda," she was saying, "the patients need attention—you'd better go. Now, remember, you're not to tell them anything—just say you don't know, no matter what they ask."

Linda said, "Yes, Miss Pane," and after settling her cap and giving her hips a wiggle she marched off.

Miss Fane looked tired and worried, and I felt sorry for her. I sat up and said, "I feel all right now, really; I can get up and look after things."

"Well—" She looked doubtful, but her voice held a note of relief. "Linda insists on staying, and if you could give her a hand, tell her what to do—you know Linda."

"It will be all right," I promised her, "We'll see to things."

She gave me a little smile and left, and I eased myself slowly off the bed. It wasn't bad; things were inclined to swing around a bit if I moved too quickly, but I felt that I could manage.

Shaw came back and, after remembering to inquire into my health, asked if I knew what had happened to William's false thumb, as it seemed to be missing.

I told him I had put it on the bureau in his room, and Shaw nodded and disappeared again.

I made my way slowly out into the corridor and came face to face with George Moon.

He said, "Hello. Shall I just start searchin' or should I waste time findin' out what the boys want me to search for?"

"I'd have given anything to see your handsome face some time ago," I said coldly, "but as far as I'm concerned at this point, you can take it home and bury it under your favorite plant."

He looked deeply pained. "That's right—blame me. George can take it—let George do it. I was racin' up here with my hair flyin' in the wind, and they go and grab me off for another job. I try tellin' them I'm needed here, but nobody gives a damn."

"Well," I said, drawing a long quivering breath, "I know one thing. Hereafter I'm going to be a day nurse or I'm not going to be a nurse at all."

Morgue, standing some distance down the corridor, waved an imperious hand at George, who shuffled off, and a moment later Shaw emerged from William's room, fingering the black thumb guard. Several men appeared from the solarium, walked up the corridor, and pushed through the hall door on their way to the elevator.

I took a few more cautious steps, which put me into a position to see the faces of Mrs. Evans and Mr. Thomas flattened against their respective windows. Ad Miller's room was lighted, but the shades were drawn, and I felt morally certain that Linda was kissing him and probably catching scarlet fever. I cursed her for a fool and rapped smartly on the door.

She peered out with her cap hanging on one ear and her face flushed. "My dear," she squeaked, "you shouldn't be on your feet with that head!"

"I tried to leave it lying on the bed," I said shortly, "but it came right along with me. Linda, must you be an ass every minute of your waking time?"

She opened her eyes very wide. "But I've attended to the others, and I don't see why I can't talk to Ad for a few minutes. He's trying to cheer me up in my sorrow."

"Does he have to have the shades drawn to cheer you up?" I asked, but she had already backed into the room again. For a second I hated Louise Fish, and then I spent three minutes wondering why she had entered my mind at all.

I tried to think of something else and oddly recalled Betty Condit having said that Mrs. Dana had made some remark to the effect that she had been exposed to what she called adult scarlet fever.

It lay passive in my mind for a moment, and then it clicked. I thought of Mrs. Evans, Mr. Thomas, and Ad Miller—and I knew that one of them was a murderer.

CHAPTER 31

I WENT slowly back to the desk, ignoring Mrs. Evans, who rapped smartly on her window to try to get my attention.

I sat down with my elbows on the desk and my head resting on my hands and thought about Mrs. Dana. She was exposed to scarlet fever, and the person was an adult; she contracted German measles and landed in the wing with the private scarlet-fever patients. But if the German measles was design and not accident how did she manage to contract it? Anyway, as soon as she was established she asked for a list of the patients in the wing and seemed satisfied when I had given it to her. Next she sang "John Brown's Body" incessantly, as she used to do at home on the first of each month. That was a signal, of course, probably an "all clear, come and see me."

That signal had been meant for Mrs. Evans, Mr. Thomas, or Ad Miller, and since she had left a description behind it should be easy to pick the right one.

Only it wasn't. If I had happened on any one of them pulling at an earlobe it would have made everything easier, and I decided to spend more time with them and concentrate on it.

My head began to swing around like a top, and I stood up and made my way unsteadily into the room I had recently occupied. I stretched out on the bed and closed my eyes, and my head stopped spinning and settled into a dull ache.

I thought of the person who had paced the vacant room next to Mrs. Evans and wondered who and why. Unless he was a red herring thrown by Mrs. Evans herself.

"Remove the frown," said the voice of Dr. Lawrence, and I opened my eyes.

"Never think as hard as that," he went on. "It's a mistake to take things too seriously. Look at Morgue. And while we're on the subject of Morgue, I don't suppose he has given a second thought to your probable headache, so I brought you something myself."

He produced a couple of pills and got me some water to wash them down, and when I choked over them he observed that that ought to make me more understanding and sympathetic with patients who found pill swallowing a little difficult.

When I had composed myself he sat down on one of the chairs and asked what had become of Linda.

"She's doing a little spadework," I said briefly.

"Spadework?"

"When Linda is faced with trouble," I explained, "she has a tremendous capacity for brushing it aside and getting on to something that she really wants to do.

"And she enjoys spadework?" he asked politely.

"Spadework is what Louise Fish did on you."

"Oh." He laughed a little. "Who's the gent?"

"It's Ad Miller," I said impatiently. "She's engaged to him."

"I don't know Ad Miller, but I should think that since a marriage has been arranged the necessity for spadework should be past. But why don't you try a little spadework on me? I'm fairly certain that that Fish could be cut out."

I shook my head. "I don't want to cause any upsets in the Fish household, and there are plenty of others who will do quite as well for me. But thanks for the invitation, anyway."

"You're too careless with your future," he said in a dissatisfied voice. "For instance, supposing you fell into the arms of Morgue on the rebound?"

"What rebound?" I asked, but I couldn't help laughing, although it hurt my head.

"Aren't you in love with me?"

"Of course, how could I help it? But I seem to be in love with my steady, too, and I get distinct twinges every time I see that nephew—you know, Gavin Bart."

"That hunk of cheese?" he said, elevating his eyebrows. "Let me warn you, girl, against long eyelashes and a straight nose. He has beauty, certainly—"

"And riches too," I said.

"That's just it." He stood up, advanced to the bed, and leaned over with purpose in his eyes, but I pushed him away.

"Don't," I said in a muffled voice. "As far as you're concerned, I could be capable even of murder. You thought so—remember?"

He straightened up again and took his cigarette case from his breast pocket. "You mean you're going to make it difficult for me?"

"Give me a cigarette," I said with a cautious glance at the door. "If you're going to smoke in here I can get in a few puffs without being found out."

He lighted a couple of cigarettes and handed one to me. He watched me while I inhaled once or twice, and then said in a satisfied voice, "Now I have you. I can blast you out of the profession for infringement of rules, and when you become indigent I'll step in and dazzle you with my riches."

I watched a smoke ring float lazily upward and said, "My steady would never allow me to become indigent."

"Anent that steady," he observed after a moment's silence. "He's getting in my hair—even more than pretty-boy Gavin."

His hair. I glanced at it and wondered idly if it were all his. I had a little lost faith in men's heads since the harrowing episode with Benny.

"Just bend over a minute, will you," I said suddenly, "and let me see the top of your head?"

He lowered his head at once. "There has been no infestation since my third year in grade school, but I wouldn't want you to take my word for it."

I gave a fistful of his hair a sharp tug, but it stayed on, and I lay back, satisfied.

He straightened up with watering eyes. " Wasn't that rather vicious?"

"Possibly," I agreed, "but I wanted to do it only once."

Shaw came in just then and sent Dr. Lawrence away. He asked me a lot of questions which I answered with my eyes closed and in which he did not seem to be much interested, anyway, and then his tone changed.

"I've checked up on all those in connection with this case in regard to that description left by Mrs. Dana. Now I want to check on the three patients who are still here."

"Did anyone fit?" I asked curiously.

"Not exactly. But these patients—what about 'slightly bald'?"

"All three," I said promptly.

"Sons?"

"Mrs. Evans and Mr. Thomas." I wrinkled my forehead. "Of course Mr. Miller might—"

He nodded. "Yes, I see. Now about pulling at the lobe of the ear?"

"I have never seen any of them do it."

"Removable bridges?"

"I don't know," I said, shaking my head. "They wash their own teeth. You see they're not ill enough—"

"No. Well, now I'd like you to do something if you feel up to it. Miss Fane and Miss Anderson are busy, and I don't want the niece on this job. I want you to go into their rooms now and settle the removable-bridge question."

I pulled myself off the bed at once, feeling flattered and important. My head bothered me hardly at all, and I nodded at Shaw and went out into the corridor. Linda was at the desk working on the charts, and I went to Ad Miller's room first because I did not know how long she was apt to leave him alone.

Gray dawn lay palely against the window, and in its light I could see that Ad had drifted off to sleep. I woke him with nursy efficiency, told him it was morning, remarked on the fact that he'd had a nice long sleep, and asked him if he didn't think it was time he sprang out of bed with a song on his lips.

He opened his eyes and regarded me languidly. "Dear heart," he said, "I have a sense of time even when I'm asleep. But I have no fight in me. What is it? Am I to be done in now?"

I shivered and whispered, "Oh, please! How can you be so flippant about it?"

"What does it matter?" he said indifferently.

"I don't know." I straightened my backbone and put some starch into my voice. "Open your mouth, please."

This inspiration had just come to me, since I had entered his room with no more brilliant idea than to ask him point-blank about his bridges or lack of them.

He gave me a sleepy, half-amused look from under half-closed lids. "I doubt your authority, and I believe you're stepping on the toes of my medical adviser, but I won't upset your pretty little plans. Enjoy yourself, lady."

He opened his mouth, and I saw at once that there were two bridges—one in the upper jaw and one in the lower. I couldn't mistake them, because Mother had a pair that were almost identical.

"All right," I said. "Close your mouth and go back to sleep."

"Thanks, yes. I believe I shall. It's kind of you people to be so attentive. I hardly think my throat could have lasted until I was awake and had had my breakfast."

I left him, gave a nod to Shaw, who was waiting in the corridor, and went on to Mr. Thomas' room.

Mr. Thomas was awake and anxious to talk.

"I couldn't sleep, Nurse—impossible—all that going on out there. There's been an accident, hasn't there?"

"Mr. Dana had an accident," I said lamely.

He continued to question me, and at last I gave him a garbled story that was part lie and part truth. He relaxed back onto his pillow then and said, "Dreadful, dreadful."

I asked him to open his mouth, and he opened it at once without curiosity, and with the apathy that some patients develop toward incomprehensible hospital routine.

But there were no removable bridges—only a gold inlay here and there.

I left him, apparently more or less eased in his mind, and went on to Mrs. Evans. She was sound asleep, probably worn out with her efforts to get someone to tell her all about it, but she did not resent being awakened. She hailed my presence with joy and satisfaction and asked me about fifty questions without stopping for breath.

When I was able to break in I requested her to open her mouth, and she was promptly diverted. She wanted to know why.

"We've lost a fly," I said, exasperated, "and I've been ordered to find it."

Unexpectedly that struck her as being funny, and she opened her mouth and shrieked with laughter. I was able to get a good look at her dental arrangements, but I drew another blank. More gold inlays, but no removable bridges.

She closed her mouth with a snap when she saw that I was looking into it, and I turned hastily away and began to scrub out. I glanced at the hall window and encountered the dark gaze of Gavin Bart, who was moodily staring into the room and absently pulling at the lobe of his ear.

CHAPTER 32

I HURRIED out, followed by a remark from Mrs. Evans to the effect that the nurses would allow a patient to die rather than pass up an opportunity to talk to a good-looking man.

Gavin had stopped pulling at his ear, and he greeted me somberly. "This is a terrible thing. I wish I could get my hands on the—"

"Hush!" I said hastily and added, "I know. I'm sorry."

He lowered his voice, "He was such a nice old bird—pathetic, in a way. I don't understand why anyone would want to harm him."

Shaw loomed up behind us and dismissed Gavin with a curt "All right, Mr. Bart. I want to speak to the nurse."

Gavin elevated his eyebrows and moved away a few paces, and Shaw turned to me.

"Well?"

"No bridges except Mr. Miller, and I guess he has no sons."

"He might have," Shaw said in a dissatisfied voice. "What about the ear pulling?"

I shook my head. "I still haven't seen any of them do it."

Shaw turned away, hesitated, and turned back again. "Could you get a look into Bart's mouth? You might give him some hogwash about precautions and communicable diseases. I'll wait up at the desk, but don't let him think I told you to do it."

I nodded and walked off feeling quite important. I supposed that Shaw had seen Gavin pulling at his ear and that he trusted me because my harrowing experience in the solarium had crossed me off the suspect list. And that despite Morgue's show-off speech that made so light of my injuries.

I approached Gavin and asked, "Would you like a cup of coffee?"

He said, "Yes, thanks," rather absently.

"Come along to the kitchen, then, and I'll make some. God knows, I need something myself."

He stopped suddenly and said in a sick voice, "Wait a minute—they're bringing him out."

I hurried to draw the blinds in the three occupied rooms and noticed that Linda, up at the desk, was crying noisily. Shaw seemed to be patting her on the back.

When the stretcher with its gruesome, sheeted burden had disappeared I lowered the blinds in the patients' rooms again and went back to the desk.

Shaw was saying to Linda, "Why don't you go off duty? I'm sure your superior—"

But Linda interrupted, "No, no—I don't want to. I can't go back to my room and just lie there thinking about it."

Gavin came forward and said in a tired voice, "Linda, suppose we forget about fighting for a while, and we'll go out and get some coffee or something."

She mopped at her eyes with a damp handkerchief and said with a childish hiccup, "We can have coffee here. I can't leave Norma now—I told Miss Fane I'd stay—and anyway, we've only a little over an hour. We can all have coffee, because there are only three patients now—"

Her voice trailed off, but before she could start crying again I urged them all into the diet kitchen and set her to making the coffee. Gavin drifted to a corner and leaned up against the wall, and I snatched at the opportunity.

"Open your mouth," I said in a low voice, "and let me look at your throat. You've been around here so much—and an ounce of prevention—"

He looked faintly surprised and said, "But I thought your beastly, barren corridors were germproof."

I gave a distinctly silly laugh and said, "Oh well, occasionally we miscue."

To my relief he lost interest and opened his mouth. I saw one small bridge in the upper jaw before I said confusedly, "You're all right," and backed away without having glimpsed at his throat.

Linda served the coffee, and Shaw gave me a potent look over the edge of his cup. I gave him a brief nod and then glanced at Gavin, feeling both mean and creepy.

His face was grim and desperately tired, and somehow I could not believe that he was responsible for all that horror. I did not see how he could have managed it, either, simply as a visitor. Of course he had been able to get in easily enough, and Mrs. Evans had complained of someone pacing the vacant room beside hers. And someone whom he probably knew had twice talked to William in the solarium. William had been shy, and I could not picture him cozily chatting to a stranger.

Shaw maneuvered me to one side and murmured, "So Miller and Bart are the only ones with bridges and Miller is slightly bald. Would you call Bart slightly bald?"

I glanced at Gavin and said, "No," doubtfully.

He noticed my indecision and went on, "You and I might conceivably bring him into the slightly bald class, but his aunt—never. She was fond of him and very proud of him. And yet he pulls at his ear."

So Shaw had seen. I nodded, feeling confused and miserable.

"You're on tomorrow night'" he asked abruptly.

"Yes."

"Then I'd like you to do something for me. Spend as much time as you can with Miller and watch for the ear-pulling business. If he's been warned about it he'd be careful not to do it in front of me or anyone who might recognize it. But it's a habit and it might reassert itself when he's relaxed."

"Well, yes," I agreed. "But he has no son."

"No telling," Shaw said, his sharp eyes gone thoughtful. "I'm going to look into it. In any case, I trust you to keep all this quiet."

I assured him I would and then turned hastily to Linda and Gavin, who were in the midst of an argument that threatened to become a disturbance of the peace.

It seemed to involve a framed painting that Linda declared had belonged to her father and which had been stolen by Aunt Aggie. Linda said she had no intention of claiming it, since she was not the type to haggle over the possessions of people hardly cold in their graves, but, nevertheless, it belonged to her father.

Gavin said that no doubt Linda's father was a very fine gentleman and all that, but there was no denying the fact that he had entered the family with one passable suit of clothes and a pocket handkerchief.

Shaw's ears began to flap, but I went in and broke it up.

"You're both showing very bad taste and you ought to be ashamed of yourselves," I said, raising my voice above theirs.

They shut up, and Linda walked away without another word. She went straight to Ad Miller's room, presumably to give him his morning bath. Shaw and Gavin went off together, and I went in to Mrs. Evans because she was awake.

"I haven't slept a wink all night," she said, as I knew she would. "I shall have a relapse if this keeps up, and you know I can't be spared at home. I want to be moved—in fact, I insist upon it."

"All right," I said agreeably. "Tell the day nurse, will you? I'm going off in a few minutes."

She changed her tone completely. "Something happened here last night, and I demand to know what it was. It was something dreadful, too, I could feel it. And why did you come rushing in and draw the blind? I still have ears, you know, and I'm sure they brought someone out of that solarium. The poor Dana man died there, didn't he? And his sister so ill. How is the sister?"

"She died," I said briefly.

"Oh, the poor man!" Mrs. Evans exclaimed in a shocked voice. "Then perhaps he died of grief. That girl Linda—the niece—told me he was very fond of his sister. But how did he get down to the solarium? A little unhinged, perhaps, looking for her."

"Sounds reasonable," I admitted, drying my hands preparatory to leaving. She gave me a suspicious look, and I fled before she could demand my version of the story.

Mr. Thomas was awake and gave me a courteous good morning. "Nurse, I want to be moved from this floor or, preferably, go home. I know they must have removed a body when you drew the blind. Well, that's reasonable, of course—people die in hospitals—but there's something going on around here. I don't understand it and I don't like it."

"It's all right, Mr. Thomas," I said inanely. "We'll take care of you."

"That's all very well," he said almost peevishly, "but you promised to keep my door locked, and then that other one came along and left it open."

"I'll lock it now," I promised, "and you remind the day nurses every time they come in."

I went out, locked the door ostentatiously, and wended my way along the corridor. I noticed that Linda was still with Ad Miller and kept my head elaborately turned away as I passed his window. Shaw and Gavin were standing close to the doors that led to the elevator and appeared to be in earnest conversation. Benny Phipps was at the desk eating peanuts.

He said, "Say! How tight was that false thumb on the guy's hand?"

I looked at him, my mind going to William and his thumb, and suddenly I dropped heavily into a chair. William was intensely sensitive about that thumb, and there must have been a considerable struggle in the corridor before he could have lost it. And the patients restless and nervous! Why, one of them must have seen that struggle; it could hardly be otherwise.

CHAPTER 33

PERHAPS TWO of the patients had seen that struggle—or all three! But I shook my head over that. It must have come out if they had all seen it. I was convinced, however, that at least one of them knew; it seemed impossible that they could all have slept through it.

I glanced up as Gavin approached the desk and dropped heavily into one of the chairs. Shaw followed slowly.

"All right," Gavin said, "I'll tell you." He pressed the back of his hand against his eyes for a moment and then stared dejectedly at the floor. "I was here that night, as apparently you know. I was worried, naturally, because I knew that Aunt Aggie had come here purposely for some devilment of her own. For years she'd been making money out of something, but she was very closemouthed about it and would not tell anyone what it was. Uncle William didn't seem to know anything and wasn't interested, anyway, as far as I could see. I've always been afraid that it was something not quite on the level, but I never bothered to push an inquiry; I just let it go.

"About two weeks ago I went out and had dinner with them. Aunt Aggie spoke of having taken some toy to a neighboring child who was confined to the house with a case of German measles. Uncle William spoke up and complained that Aggie had dragged him along, too, had kissed the child good-by, and made him kiss it as well. I was not interested at the time, but when I heard from Jim Lawrence that they were both in the hospital with something that had turned out to be German measles I began to wonder. Jim said that Aunt Aggie had insisted upon going to the hospital before it was possible to be sure of the diagnosis, and. I remembered Linda having said, in front of us all, that cases of German measles sometimes got in through mistaken diagnosis and were often put in a scarlet-fever wing. Jim told me that Aunt Aggie had declared she'd been exposed to scarlet fever and was probably coming down with it. She made a great fuss about being put in with the private scarlet-fever patients, and Jim arranged it all. He phoned me afterward and said that it was damned queer she'd want to spend money on a hospital.

"I knew then that she'd done the whole thing on purpose and had taken Uncle William with her because he'd always been a bit weak-minded, and she'd always taken care of him and didn't want to leave him alone.

"I was worried about the whole thing, and after I had visited her the next evening I slipped into a vacant room while Norma wasn't looking.

"I'll never forget that night, either. I wanted to wait until they had all been bedded down and everything was quiet, and then I intended to slip into Aunt Aggie's room and have it out with her. In the meantime I lay down on the bed and went to sleep.

"It was very quiet when I woke up. I looked out, found the corridor deserted and no one at the desk, and I slipped across to Aunt Aggie's room without being seen. I broke one of the cardinal laws and went straight in, but I did not put on the light. I spoke to her several times but could not get any answer, and at last I switched on my pocket flashlight.

"I'll never forget it—her—the way she looked. I tell you, I almost fainted. I ran out, and I suppose I left the door open. I was thinking only of giving the alarm. But I heard someone coming and I realized that I had no business to be there, so I ducked back into the vacant room.

"I heard the uproar start and flourish and I knew that it would not be long before the rooms were searched. I had put myself into a questionable position, to say the least, and I knew that things would be pretty bad for me if I were found. There were people coming and going in the corridor, and at last I took the plunge, pulled my hat down over my eyes, and walked out. Some of the personnel of the police force had forgotten to remove their hats, so I looked like one of the boys. I walked briskly down the corridor to the solarium and hid myself in the darkest corner. It seemed as though I had been there for hours, when the light was suddenly snapped on and Uncle William walked in. He pulled two chairs up to a window and stretched out with his feet and legs on one and the rest of him on the other. It did not look like a very comfortable arrangement, but he appeared to be quite relaxed.

"I did not want him to see me, but I had been so surprised at his entrance that I had come out a little way, and before I could back up I saw his head jerk around to me.

"He said, 'Oh, Gavin, it's a good thing you came. Something awful has happened to Aggie. I knew it would someday—she was always doing things. They took her away—she's dead. She died tonight.'

"I told him that he was not supposed to leave his room and that he'd better go back before he was caught. He demurred a bit, but I got him out into the corridor, which was empty, and finally to his room. I had to hide in my vacant room again and I paced the floor, wondering what on earth to do next and expecting to be discovered at any minute. Just before seven, when Norma was busy with one of the patients, I took a chance and simply walked out of the place. No one stopped me, and I went on home, where I was given the news of my aunt's death, and so had to come straight back here again."

Gavin paused at this point. Shaw muttered something about a shake-up in his department, and Benny went pale.

Gavin shifted his position and went on, "The thing that bothered me was that chair being chopped. As soon as I heard of it I suspected Uncle William, because I knew he loved to chop wood, and on two occasions, when there had been no logs or kindling wood for him, he had gone to work on some old pieces of furniture in the cellar. I was very worried, because Aunt Aggie had mentioned from time to time that she had a little hatchet with which to protect herself should it ever become necessary. I never actually believed her until I heard of that chair being chopped, and then I went into a cold sweat. I supposed she had taken the damned thing to the hospital with her and that Uncle William had managed to get hold of it. I searched the entire wing, with the exception of the patients' rooms, but I never found it. And then when the second chair was chopped I was fit to break a blood vessel."

"Did it never occur to you to give your information to the police?" Shaw snapped. "You might have saved your uncle's life."

Gavin looked mildly surprised and said easily, "No, you can't say that. You never found the hatchet, you know, and of course you should have. I was afraid if I told you that you'd think Uncle William had killed Aunt Aggie, and he'd always been such a harmless old soul. I was trying to protect him."

Shaw appeared to be just about at the boiling point, and it was with profound relief that I saw Betty Condit heading for the desk. Linda had come up, and we handed the wing over to Betty with an expression of sorrow, from me, that we could not put it on a plate and garnish it with parsley. "But it's yours," I said earnestly, "and don't bother to thank us."

I herded Linda down to the dining room and made her order coffee and something to eat, although she was shedding tears again.

Miss Fane came up to us presently and, after a perfunctory word of condolence to Linda, examined my head while I ate some toast.

"Do you have to jump your scalp around like that?" she asked impatiently.

I stopped crunching, and after a while she said she thought my head would be the same as ever, and what with my youth and a good sleep, I could go on duty again that night.

I nodded sadly, and she went off. Linda and I finished breakfast and made our way to the nurses' home almost in silence. Linda had dried off again and looked quite happy, and I supposed she was thinking of Ad.

She wanted to come into my room and chat for a while, but my head was aching and I put her off. Which was just as well, as it happened, because when I got in there myself I found Dr. Lawrence sitting on a chair, waiting for me.

CHAPTER 34

"GET OUT of here," I whispered. "Quickly. Do you know what will happen if you're found here?"

He nodded. "That Fish will break her engagement with me, and you'll be fired out of the hospital. Not undesirable situations, as things stand."

"Stop horsing," I said, still whispering, "and for God's sake, get out."

He hauled out a cigarette and said, "No. I want a few words with you."

I removed my cap and shoes, hurled them into different corners of the room, and flopped onto the bed.

"I'm disappointed in you," he said after a moment. "I supposed you'd be thrilled when you walked in and found me here—and instead of that all you can think of is what the neighbors will say."

"Let's get down to brass tacks," I suggested. "The sooner you get out of here the sooner I can start breathing again."

He rose from the chair and after fooling around for a moment approached the bed, carrying a paper cup with a pill in one hand and a glass of water in the other. "Guaranteed to produce sleep. Some earnest research artist derived a lot of satisfaction from the discovery of this stuff, some drug house a lot of money, and you get a sound sleep. There's a deal of melancholy refection to be had out of all that."

I took the pill because he looked as though he might be stubborn about it.

He returned to the chair and arranged himself comfortably in it. "That will keep you out of mischief for a while, so that when I return I won't find you playing around with Gavin or Morgue or anyone else. I have a busy day before me, prefaced by a visit to Louise Fish. I intend to break our engagement—unless her mother is there, of course—but I should be able to get her alone sometime."

"Don't be too hasty," I said coldly. "Better not cast off one woman before you're sure you have another lined up."

He said, "I have," and left his chair again. I saw it coming, but I wasn't able to push him away before he had kissed me three times with a good deal of vigor.

When I had the use of my mouth again I started. "If you think—" But he interrupted me.

He kissed me again before I could duck and then went to the door and, peering out cautiously, slipped into the hall and closed it behind him. I felt morally certain that several of the girls were peeking through cracks in their doors, but I was too tired to care.

My mind drifted to Gavin's story, and I decided that he had been telling the truth. Mrs. Dana, then, had wangled her way into the hospital purposely and had signaled to one of the patients already there by singing "John Brown's Body." Whoever recognized the signal had known where the hatchet was hidden and had gone in and got rid of Mrs. Dana forever. William knew about the hatchet, too—liked to play with it. But what quarrel did he have with anyone? And why had he not mentioned the fact that he knew one of the patients? Obviously because he did not know, as his sister had known, that that person was a patient.

I turned over restlessly. William must have found out that that familiar person had a room in the wing and so had to be killed before he could mention it, in mild surprise, to one of the doctors or nurses. Probably he had made his discovery on a trip down to the solarium, and the struggle had taken place immediately because of the pressing need to silence him before he could talk to anyone.

Apparently he had decided to sneak a visit to the solarium when Linda had forgotten to relock his door. The hatchet had been taken from the spare room and used in the dreadful struggle that ended up in the solarium.

I felt convinced that one of the remaining two patients had witnessed the struggle. I did not think that both of them would have kept it quiet, but there might have been some reason for one of them to remain silent. Blackmail, perhaps.

At that point, quite suddenly, I fell asleep, and the unknown research artist had done his work so well that I was out cold until five o'clock. I had not slept so late for many a day, and I had to fly around a bit to get things done. I left the building at a few minutes past six and was nabbed on the bottom step by Dr. Lawrence, who seemed to have lost his cheerful impertinence and was scowling instead.

"Hurry," he said shortly. "You haven't much time." He took my arm and ran me over to his car instead of in the direction of the main building.

"Listen—wait a minute," I said loudly. "I have to eat."

He practically pushed me into the front seat and slammed the door on me, and a minute or so later we shot down the driveway and out into the street.

"Don't you ever think of anything but food?" he asked presently. "No wonder I can't make the grade. All I ever get is a smile or two directly after feeding hours."

"That'll teach you to take the Fish and me for granted," I murmured, leaning back and enjoying the breeze he was producing by breaking the speed limit.

We presently pulled up at a tearoom that the girls often used when they wanted to get out and had nowhere to go.

"I'm in an evil mood," he said as we went in. "Those clucks are not a step farther along in solving this thing. Shaw has a face as long as a horse, and Benny walks around as though the floor were made of eggs and even went so far as to remark that, after all, a patrolman's uniform certainly did things for a guy. What will you have?"

I ordered and then sat back and gloomily considered another night in that hateful wing.

Dr. Lawrence sat in restless silence for a while and then said, "We could have cleared the whole mess if we'd called the police and had a thorough search made when we found that the hatchet was missing from that false bottom. Somebody had it, then, waiting."

I nodded somberly. "If you hadn't butted in when I was looking through the bag that first time— It must still have been there, then."

"I know—and poor old William might have been saved. But it was such a shock to me when I came along and saw you pawing through the thing because I had just figured that there must be a false bottom or a flexible lining. I was on my way to William's room to verify it, and there you were in that vacant room. You can imagine what I thought and I really thought it too—and my one idea was to get you away. Later, when I found the bag empty, I thought you must have hidden the hatchet somewhere else. Of course after you were conked, and all the rest of it, I knew you were completely innocent. And by the way, how long are you going to be mad at me for all this?"

I had eaten all that a suddenly deflated appetite could stand, and I got up and left the place. Dr. Lawrence hurriedly paid the bill and followed me, and as he pushed me into the car he said, "I've no doubt you entertained a few suspicions of me along the way too."

Well, that was true, and I could not deny it.

"So I ask you again," he went on, "how long it will be before your mad begins to lift."

"Don't expect anything under a week," I said coldly.

"Then how about deferring the beginning until tomorrow? Because I have to sit with you all night, and I'm a chatty soul."

I felt a rush of cool relief, since I had expected to be guarded only by Benny, who was somewhat of a broken reed. But I said merely, "I doubt if you'll be permitted—"

"All arranged with Shaw and Fane," he broke in amiably. "Miss Fane had a few doubts, so I told her in the strictest confidence that we were engaged, and that cleared her up at once."

I gritted my teeth and said furiously, "I'll send her a message immediately asking to have you removed—by force, if necessary."

He laughed. "No, you won't. It was the truth, because all our difficulties have been smoothed away. I jilted the Fish this afternoon—such a scene. Not that you could blame her; I'm such a catch. Hundred and fifty in the bank—or it will be when I deposit the fifty cents I got for fee splitting—hardly any dependents, only Grandpa and Aunt Ruby. Cousin Joe isn't a full-time dependent—only during those periods after they spring him and before they catch him. Now if you'll have a look in my right-hand pocket, you'll find the engagement ring that I wrested from L. Fish. I nearly pulled her finger off, but I got it—and it's all yours."

He drew up at the hospital entrance, and I got out without a word and mounted the steps while he swung off toward the parking space.

I found Betty looking tired and exasperated. "I've had to scrub that Shaw and myself in and out of those three rooms so many times it's a wonder we have any skin left. And the patients are so nervous they couldn't eat any supper. How can the man think up so many questions? They all three look fit to have relapses tonight."

"All right," I said resignedly, "let 'em blow. I can always commit suicide."

Betty presently went off, and immediately Shaw was at my side. He spoke almost without moving his lips.

"Miller has a son."

CHAPTER 35

I DIGESTED this for a moment and then—I think to Shaw's annoyance—I said, "The cad!" and burst out laughing.

He shrugged the flippancy aside and said, "Spend as much time as you can in his room tonight, will you? If he pulls at the lobe of his ear just once I'll arrest him anyway." His face settled into lines of gloom, and he added bitterly, "I've never run across anything so difficult in my life—having to be degermed and hung up to dry every time I question someone."

"You ought to go home and take a rest," I said sympathetically.

He shook his head. "I've forgotten what my home looks like. I'm spending the night in the solarium and I intend to do some thinking. Phipps is spending the night in the diet kitchen, and Dr. Lawrence, at his own insistence, is spending the night at your desk." His face relaxed into a faint smile. "The doctor probably expects to have a lot of your company, but that's where he's wrong, because I'll expect you to give every spare minute to Miller."

"Every spare second," I amended firmly.

He must have expected me to be disappointed because he looked at me oddly for a moment and then shrugged and turned away. He wandered up and down the corridor a couple of times, snooping into the patients' windows, and then disappeared rather abruptly into the solarium.

I decided to attend to Mrs. Evans and Mr. Thomas first and then fix up Ad Miller and linger as long as possible afterward. I put aside firmly a sudden uncomfortable thought of Linda and set to work.

I went into Mrs. Evans first and was not surprised to find her highly excited.

"They've been asking me questions," she said shrilly, "all sorts of questions—and I found out all about it. They were *murdered,* and you never told me. You talked about complications and relapses. I've been deceived and lied to."

"I'm sorry, Mrs. Evans," I said, rattling basins efficiently, "but I must obey orders, you know. I have to say what I'm told to say."

"Well, I suppose so," she conceded. "But it wasn't right, all the same. My husband would never have allowed me to stay here for a *minute* if he'd known."

"I'm sure he wouldn't," I agreed warmly and wondered whether Mr. Evans ever had any say about anything.

She calmed down after that, and I was able to get out without any trouble.

Mr. Thomas expressed himself as being profoundly shocked. "Dreadful—really dreadful. It's almost unbelievable. I knew there was something, of course—I said so. But you'd think the police—"

This type of thing went on until I had finished with him, when I advised him to try to relax and get to sleep.

I crossed the corridor and walked up toward Ad's room. Dr. Lawrence waved to me from his seat at the desk, but I ignored him and went into Ad with my chin in the air.

Ad was cheerful, and I felt a corresponding gloom as I thought of how close he was to trouble and how little he seemed to realize it.

"Out into the dizzy whirl again this afternoon, we forgathered in the solarium as usual. Tell me, sweet—and don't flinch, because I can take it—do you think Linda and I will ever become such as Evans and Thomas?"

" No," I said dryly. "You'll both be working to hang onto your youth instead of boasting about your children—if any."

"The session was chaperoned by a policeman today," he went on, "a large policeman who had a certain amount of difficulty in trying to pretend that he was not there. He was out in the hall, of course, but he glued a big red ear to the glass. Gave me quite a start—I thought it was a crayfish at first."

"Did he get anything for his trouble?" I asked, trying to be careless and feeling uncomfortably like a spy.

Ad laughed. "It was a lovely conversation. Mrs. Evans retold the story of her appendectomy because she'd forgotten a few important points the first three times. Mr. Thomas told us again of the time he was runner-up in the club golf championship. Such a pity—just as he was about to make the important putt he remembered forgetting to tell his wife not to use the car because it had developed intestinal trouble and should go in for repairs."

"Too bad about you," I said, splashing water around in the basin. "What did you tell them?"

He folded his arms behind his head and sighed. "It's catching, sweet, that sort of thing. I don't deny it, and I'll admit quite frankly that I told them about the time I had two teeth pulled. You can laugh and you can say what you like, but still and all it's a better story than either of theirs."

I sniffed. "No kidding! You must tell it to me sometime. Not now, though, because I'm not in the mood. Incidentally, weren't they jealous? How are their teeth?"

"They were green," he said, smiling at the ceiling. "Mr. Thomas hasn't been to a dentist for years—teeth all perfectly sound. Mrs. Evans spoke feebly of a gold inlay or two, but she knew she was worsted."

"When are you and Linda going to be married?" I asked, trying to make conversation.

"Dear heart, how can I tell you until Linda tells me?"

"Rubbish!" I said tartly. "You must have some say in the matter."

He cocked an eye at me and said, "Not at all. Linda is in charge of all arrangements. My only stipulation is that I remain in my apartment because I like it. If she wants to come and live with me there she's quite welcome."

"Is that how your proposal was worded?"

"Yes, it was, and she agreed, and then when it was all fixed up about her staying with me during her off hours she says casually that we might as well go through the marriage ceremony, because her aunt might find out, otherwise, and cut her out of her will. She said the ceremony wouldn't be binding if we ever wanted to change our minds, because there was always Reno."

"And now that her aunt is dead?"

"Don't be silly," said Ad. "If she could think up something the first time she could do it again. I'm hooked and I know it."

I laughed and began to scrub out. I was afraid he'd be suspicious if I stayed any longer and I knew that if he was going to pull absentmindedly at his ear he'd never do it if he were suspicious.

I went along to the desk and found Dr. Lawrence slumped down in his chair, fast asleep. I ignored him and got to work on the charts. Time passed on, and Dr. Lawrence began to snore faintly. I resisted several bright ideas and left him alone.

It was almost time for Linda to appear, when a thought came to me that excited me to a point where I had to act on it at once.

I went quietly along to Ad's room and found him awake and disposed to be amiable.

"Darling," he said, "the more I see you the better I like you. Won't you marry me as well?"

"I'd love to. And Linda and I get along well too."

"Then it's settled. We can have a sort of double wedding."

"Listen, Ad," I said eagerly. "Did Mrs. Evans and Mr. Thomas speak to each other privately this afternoon?"

"No, sweet, they did not. I should be less exhausted now if they had."

I fooled around, tidying the already tidy room, and presently I asked, "Did either of them have a piece of paper at any time?"

"Why, yes," he said with faint surprise. "Mrs. Evans had a piece of note paper or something folded up in her hand for some time. I remember she was worrying it. But whither are we drifting?"

"Did she put it away finally?" I persisted.

"I don't know—I didn't notice. Er—I think we're about to have company."

I glanced up as Linda came into the room and gave me somewhat of a cold, fishy eye.

"You could easily be jealous," Ad volunteered. "She's been in here all evening."

I went out, and Linda followed promptly. She wasted no words but asked simply, "What's the idea?"

My mind darted around in search of an explanation, and at the same time my eyes fell on the sleeping form of Dr. Lawrence.

"That's it," I said with a scornful gesture. "I was trying to make him jealous."

"Oh." She showed complete understanding and agreement at once. "Yes, I see. Is he being difficult?"

"A little."

Before I left I went down to the solarium and had a few words with Shaw. He sat up and took notice, although he mentioned the fact that he thought I was a fool.

I went off the floor, ate, showered, slept fitfully, and returned a little early.

Linda complained of headache and went off at once. Dr. Lawrence woke up and reproachfully asked me why I had gone off without letting him know. I turned my back on him and went down to the solarium.

"Nothing's happened," Shaw said aggrievedly. "How could it, anyway, with eagle eyes all over the wing?"

"I'm going into the diet kitchen," I said, "and I'll take Dr. Lawrence with me. We'll wake Benny, and the three of us will have coffee."

Shaw stood up, and I could see his eyes gleaming in the darkness. He said, "Right. And don't any of you come out of that kitchen unless you hear something."

I walked quickly, back to the desk, where I hung a sweet smile on my face and asked Dr. Lawrence if he'd like some coffee.

He stood up, creaking a little and making faces of pain. After he had slapped a cramp out of his leg he said mildly, "I believe you've forgiven me."

"Maybe." I turned my head toward the corridor and raised my voice a little. "I know it's early, but let's have coffee, anyway. I could do with some."

He gave me an owlish stare and asked, "Are you talking to me?"

I hastily put my hand on his arm and pressed it, and he fell silent. I stood for a moment watching the empty corridor. There had been no movement, but I thought one of the doors was open just a crack. It was hardly noticeable, and I wondered how many times before that door had stood the way it was now.

We went into the diet kitchen, where Benny appeared to be sleeping on his feet. He was propped against a wall with his eyes staring into space. Dr. Lawrence walked up to within a few inches of him and said, "Boo!"

Benny jumped and snarled, "What's the matter with you, guy?"

I began to fumble around with the coffee things while I strained my ears for any sound from the corridor.

Dr. Lawrence watched me for a while and said, "Let the coffee go and tell me what's on your mind."

"Not with Benny here," I murmured.

And then it came—Mrs. Evans' shrill, terrified scream.

CHAPTER 36

I COULD not keep up with Benny and Dr. Lawrence; I had to run after them.

Mrs. Evans' door was wide open, and she was sitting up in bed, her eyes wild and glittering with fear. Shaw was hanging onto Mr. Thomas, who stood impassively in his hospital pajamas.

Benny thudded over and relieved Shaw of Mr. Thomas, and Dr. Lawrence looked around at me. "So this is what you were cooking up!"

Mrs. Evans got her breath then and began to yell. "Tried to strangle me—marched right through that door and tried to strangle me!"

Shaw broke in on her and snapped, "Nurse, fix her up and then lock her door."

"Lock my door!" Mrs. Evans shrilled. "Why? What for?"

"Accessory," said Shaw and walked out of the room.

Benny and Dr. Lawrence followed, and, perforce, Mr. Thomas. I called weakly, "What about the germs?" But no one took the slightest notice.

I hastily attended to Mrs. Evans, who had calmed down and kept asking me in a frightened voice what accessory meant. I told her evasively that I did not know and presently left over her vigorous protests. I carefully locked her door and flew along to Mr. Thomas' room, where the gang had collected—still indifferent to the possibility of infection. Mr. Thomas was back in bed, and I automatically set about making him comfortable.

He was saying, "Don't be a damned fool. I know when I'm caught. It doesn't matter whether I say anything or not. But damn all women in business."

I had finished with his bed and, thoughtlessly dropping back into routine, I asked him if he'd like me to comb his hair.

He patiently begged me not to be any more of an ass than I could help and then, seeming to ignore all, of us, he began to talk with his eyes on the ceiling.

"I hate business dealings with a woman, but in the early days Mrs. Dana's setup was too good to pass by. She made the stuff and I distributed it—not locally, either. I've kept myself so well covered that no one has ever been able to connect me up."

Shaw grunted affirmatively, and Mr. Thomas went on talking to the ceiling.

"When prohibition went out we had to close down. I was satisfied, because my law practice was picking up and I was engaged to my present wife, who has influential relatives. I had left Eleanor, my first wife, and supposed I had shaken her for all time, but she caught up with me and followed me out to Mrs. Dana's house. She rang the bell while we were in the cellar, and Mrs. Dana went to the door, and the next thing they were both downstairs with me—Mrs. Dana demanding to know why I had not told her I was married, and Eleanor quietly taking in all the damning evidence that was spread around.

"Eleanor and I went out the back way and across the fields to the highway—my usual way of exit—and I admitted the spot on which she had me by asking straight out what she wanted. She replied bluntly that I was to come back and live with her or she'd expose me. I came back with an offer of a fat monthly allowance if she would divorce me. She laughed and assured me that I'd be giving her a fat monthly allowance in any case, and she added a nasty warning against any hopes for a second marriage, since she had no intention of allowing a divorce.

"I saw red, and before I knew what I was doing I had laid her head open with a stone and left her for dead. I read in the papers that she was still breathing when she was found and she was taken to a hospital. Some weeks later she was removed to the insane asylum. The newspapers said that her brain had been permanently injured, and apparently she had not had enough sense left to tell on me. She had been working in an office, using her maiden name, and I had changed my name and discarded my old friends when I started practicing law, so that my connection with Eleanor was never discovered.

"But Mrs. Dana read the newspapers, too, and she was able to put two and two together. She told me, without making any bones about it, that she wanted a certain sum every month and then advised me to go ahead and marry again, since she figured no one would be any the wiser.

"I decided to follow her advice, but I always had it in my mind to dispose of her some way. She must have known it, too, because she warned me that she had my description put away somewhere and that I should certainly be caught if I tried to serve her as I had served Eleanor.

"She forced me to come to her house once a month and bring the money in cash, and she'd sit on the porch and sing 'John Brown's Body' when the coast was clear and her dimwit brother in bed. She always insisted that I came in and chat for a while an these occasions, and one night the brother wandered out of his room and saw me. I kicked up the devil of a row because I'd always been so careful, but Mrs. Dana assured me that he'd never remember me and added that she'd only to spill a little water in front of his door to keep him from ever roaming out again while I was there. He had some sort of abnormal fear of water and an absolute horror of getting his feet wet. She must have fixed him, after that, because I did not see him at the house again.

"She always served some sort of refreshment while I was there, and while she was preparing it in the kitchen I took the opportunity to search for my description, but I could not find it. I supposed, after a while, that she had the thing in her safe-deposit box, and I began to give up the idea of disposing of her. The amount I paid her was not excessive; and I was forced to see her only once a month, so that the situation could have been worse. But I dislike blackmail, and of course her knowledge was always a cloud over my head.

"About a year ago I stumbled onto something by accident. She had suggested that we go down to the cellar and take a look at the old still. I was uninterested, but I went along, and she became almost sentimental over the thing, said she missed it, and started a lengthy explanation about how it worked. I wandered away and took a look around the cellar, and I found that framed description hanging on the wall. I read it through quickly and hastily rejoined Mrs. Dana, who was still talking and apparently too absorbed to notice that I had ever walked away from her.

"I thought it all over that night and decided to leave the description where it was and make myself over so that it no longer fitted me—in fact, to make that description into an alibi for myself.

"I was rapidly becoming a good deal more than slightly bald and I went to an out-of-town dentist and had my removable bridges made permanent. I'd never gone to the family dentist, in any case—I'd told my wife that my teeth were all right because I did not want her or anyone else to know how much money I actually have. There are several expenses of that sort that I am able to manage quietly.

"I worked long and hard on my habit of pulling at my ear; it was absurdly difficult, but I did conquer it in the end. That was about all I could do—and I was ready—but I was still worried. I was afraid she must have another description of me somewhere—probably my name, address, and occupation. I began to doubt, however, that it was in her safe-deposit vault—or why would she feel the need for that vague description in the cellar? I was still pondering on the whole thing when I came down with scarlet fever and was shipped over here.

"And then, lying here one night, I heard her hateful voice singing 'John Brown's Body.' It was very faint, and at first I thought I must be delirious, but the wretched thing persisted, and at last I got up and opened my door just a crack. There was no doubt about it—she'd got in somehow. At first I supposed she'd caught scarlet fever from me, since I'd seen her only a short time before I came down with it. Then I remembered one of the nurses mentioned a German measles patient and I realized it must be she. The coincidence of us both landing in the same hospital at the same time was so strange that I began to be suspicious. And yet if she had got herself in deliberately—why?

"It came to me after a while. She thought I might be going to die and she wanted a last whacking big sum of money.

"I spent most of that night with my door slightly open until the fuss about the chair being chopped up. I heard that that crazy Caddock had done it and was missing, and it seemed the perfect opportunity. I did not know what Caddock had used on the chair, but my weapon would be Mrs. Dana's own hatchet. I was sure she had brought the carpetbag, since she always took it with her when she stayed anywhere overnight.

"I fixed her the following night. I knew that nurse who is engaged to the Miller fellow would be in his room for some time—she always was——so I waited until she went in there and then slipped across to Mrs. Dana's room. Luckily she was asleep, and the carpetbag was lying open beside the bed. It amused me to think that she had been calling me and calling me and now that I had come she was asleep. I supposed she had discovered I was convalescing or she would have come to me.

"I don't think I'd have done it even then, except that I found the other description. I looked through the carpetbag and then in her purse, and there it was. Just my name and address with a few very enlightening words.

"I did the job the way I thought the crazy chair chopper would do it, and then I replaced the hatchet and returned to my room. I flushed her revealing notation down the toilet and felt comfortably sure that no one had seen anything. There was nothing to trouble me until early the next night when I looked up and saw William Dana staring through my window. And I had not recovered from the shock of seeing him when he opened my door and walked in. I lay here frozen, unable to speak. And while I'm on this subject, I don't mind saying that I think it shows incompetence and shiftlessness when imbecile inmates can walk into a decent patient's room at will."

Mr. Thomas paused to frown over this thought, and I caught sight of Benny's eyes bulging in utter astonishment. I felt hysterical laughter bubbling in my throat, and I stared rigidly at the floor for three full minutes.

"I thought he was going to attack me," Mr. Thomas went on, still indignant, "but all he said was, 'Hot, isn't it?'

"I said yes, it was.

"Then he asked, 'Don't I know you?'

"I told him I didn't think so, and he looked at me for a while and said he was almost sure he'd seen me somewhere—he thought with Aggie.

"I denied it, and he said good-by pleasantly and went out.

"I was very much worried because I could not feel sure that he was as vague as he seemed.

"I remembered Mrs. Dana's trick of spilling water in front of his door to keep him in his room, and since he was right next to me I tried it. It seemed to work as long as no one interfered, but the nurses kept wiping it up. I asked to have my door locked, and that was all right until that flighty little blonde forgot it. I don't know whether William was watching for something like that—or just lucky—but he came in, and this time he was carrying that hatchet with all the dried blood on it.

"He stood at the end of my bed and said, 'I know now; I guess you killed poor Aggie with this—see? It's all bloody. I didn't see the blood when I took it out before, because it was so dark. It was dark all the time—I couldn't even see where I was going.'

"I didn't know what he was talking about, but I was afraid he meant business and I began to edge out of bed. He got excited and told me to get back into bed, and then he lunged at me with the hatchet.

"I ran out into the hall, thinking that if we were discovered I might be able to shift the blame to him. He flung after me and we struggled, and then I got away and ran down to the solarium. I stood just inside the door and tripped him up when he came plunging through. He fell on the hatchet and made a nasty gash in his forehead, and I pulled him over to the wall and finished him. I thought it would be as well to close his mouth forever, but I shouldn't have done it—I might have known that someone would see us.

"I had to remove the fingerprints from the hatchet, replace it in the bag, and get back to my room—all without being seen. It wasn't easy, either. I'd like to see any of you do it. At first the nurse and that fellow were in the hall, and then the nurse by herself. She picked up the old man's false thumb and presently went to the telephone, but she was watching the corridor all the time. She walked halfway down, changed her mind and went back, and finally disappeared into the diet kitchen. It was my opportunity to replace the hatchet in the bag, and I crept up to William Dana's room—only to find that the bag was not there. I ran across to Aggie's room and found the door open, but the bag was not there, either. I got into a bit of a panic and flew into a couple of vacant rooms to search, but I didn't locate the right one. I slipped into my own room just as the nurse came out of the kitchen. I saw that she was going in to each patient, so I got into bed, put the hatchet under the bed, and snored for her when she looked in on me.

"When she left I crept to the window and looked after her, and to my horror I saw that she was on her way to the solarium. I could not have an alarm raised until I had properly disposed of the hatchet, so I followed her quietly while she hummed a tune and hit her when she got there.

"I decided to wipe off the handle of the damned hatchet and drop it anywhere. I went into a vacant room for that purpose, and there was the blasted bag sitting on the floor. I fixed up the hatchet, replaced it, and returned to my room.

"But that ass, Mrs. Evans, saw our struggle—apparently she was the only one—and today she tried to cash in on it. Resorting to a vulgar, depraved thing like blackmail, mind you, and asking for one hundred and fifty dollars! Good God! I could write a check for fifty thousand! Anyway, I wouldn't tolerate any more blackmail, so I put her note down the toilet and decided to put an end to the story of her appendectomy once and for all."

There was a short silence, and then Dr. Lawrence stirred and moved quietly to my side. He drew me out into the corridor and murmured, "I've heard all I want—and he looks fit to go on for half an hour."

"He made a mistake, you know," I said thoughtfully. "He told Ad and Mrs. Evans that his teeth never needed attention and that he had not been to a dentist for years—and yet I'd seen several gold inlays. I realized that he could have had his bridges made into the permanent type and I figured, too, that if anyone had seen the struggle in the hall he or she probably was holding out for blackmail. Ad said that Mrs. Evans was fingering a piece of paper in the solarium this afternoon, and I decided that it could be a blackmail note which she had received or intended to deliver. In any case, someone was in danger, so I told Shaw and arranged for us to be out of the way while he watched from the solarium."

"Brilliant," said Dr. Lawrence admiringly. "Tell me more. Why did William chop up the chairs?"

"It was one of his hobbies; he was a little cracked, poor soul. If he could not get firewood to chop he was apt to start on the furniture. The first time, he must have sneaked into Mrs. Dana's room and taken the hatchet—I suppose while she was asleep. I guess he kept it in his room for some time until he got a chance to go down to the solarium. He had himself a good time chopping up the chair and returned to his room, complete with hatchet. He didn't try to replace the wretched thing until much later—after I had unlocked his door and was watching George search the solarium. He must have awakened Aggie that time, and she followed him out into the hall. She was very much upset, but she didn't tell on him.

"His second spree was when all the lights went out, when he just fumbled around until he found a chair to his liking."

"Very interesting example of a lame brain," said Dr. Lawrence. "I'll have to discuss it with Morgue sometime."

"He was not as completely vague as you might suppose, though," I said thoughtfully. "For instance, he was very distressed when Mrs. Dana sang that song and seemed to be onto the fact that she was up to no good. Also, when they took her away he stood there and said, 'Have they found out?' so that he must have known she was running afoul of the law. On the other hand, when he visited the solarium after she was dead, he politely pulled up an extra chair for her and then put his feet up on it."

"So that no one else would take it before she got there, no doubt," said Dr. Lawrence. "Well, I think I'll get along and tell the Fish all about it."

"Be sure you don't leave anything out," I said agreeably. "Good night."

He took five steps down the corridor and then turned around and came back. "What's the matter with you, anyway?" he asked aggrievedly. "Why didn't you call me back? Didn't your mother ever teach you anything about holding your man?"

"Certainly," I said with dignity. "I majored in it at her insistence. But she always told me to wish the men Godspeed on their way; she claimed they were too conceited to stand that, so they always came back. After that she said I'd be able to do what I pleased with them."

"Oh, all right," he said, "I give up. I'll let Louise marry that other James Lawrence—the one she's engaged to—and you go ahead and do what you please with me. I wouldn't want to let your mother down."

THE END

About The Rue Morgue Press

The Rue Morgue vintage mystery line is designed to bring back into print those books that were favorites of readers between the turn of the century and the 1960s. The editors welcome suggests for reprints. To receive our catalog or make suggestions, write The Rue Morgue Press, P.O. Box 4119, Boulder, Colorado (1-800-699-6214). The Rue Morgue Press tries to keep all of its titles in print, though some books may go temporarily out of print for up to six months. The following list details the titles available as of June 2002.

Catalog of Rue Morgue Press titles June 2002

Titles are listed by author. All books are quality trade paperbacks measuring 6 by 9 inches, usually with full-color covers and printed on paper designed not to yellow or deteriorate. These are permanent books.

Joanna Cannan. The books by this English writer are among our most popular titles. Modern reviewers favorably compared our two Cannan reprints with the best books of the Golden Age of detective fiction. "Worthy of being discussed in the same breath with an Agatha Christie or a Josephine Tey."—Sally Fellows, Mystery News. "First-rate Golden Age detection with a likeable detective, a complex and believable murderer, and a level of style and craft that bears comparison with Sayers, Allingham, and Marsh."—Jon L. Breen, *Ellery Queen's Mystery Magazine*. Set in the late 1930s in a village that was a fictionalized version of Oxfordshire, both titles feature young Scotland Yard inspector Guy Northeast. *They Rang Up the Police* (0-915230-27-5, 156 pages, $14.00) and *Death at The Dog* (0-915230-23-2, 156 pages, $14.00).

Glyn Carr. The author is really Showell Styles, one of the foremost English mountain climbers of his era as well as one of that sport's most celebrated historians. Carr turned to crime fiction when he realized that mountains provided an ideal setting for committing murders. The 15 books featuring Shakespearean actor Abercrombie "Filthy" Lewker are set on peaks scattered around the globe, although the author returned again and again to his favorite climbs in Wales, where his first mystery, published in 1951, *Death on Milestone Buttress* (0-915230-29-1, 187 pages, $14.00), is set. Lewker is a marvelous Falstaffian character whose exploits have been praised by such discerning critics as Jacques Barzun and Wendell Hertig Taylor in *A Catalogue of Crime*. Other critics have been just as kind: "You'll get a taste of the Welsh countryside, will encounter names replete with consonants, will be exposed to numerous snippets from Shakespeare and will find Carr's novel a worthy representative of the cozies of two generations ago."—*I Love a Mystery.*

Clyde B. Clason. Clason has been praised not only for his elaborate plots and skillful use of the locked room gambit but also for his scholarship. He may be one of the few mystery authors—and no doubt the first—to provide a full bibliography of his sources. *The Man from Tibet* (0-915230-17-8, 220 pages, $14.00) is one of his best (selected in 2001 in *The History of Mystery* as one of the 25 great amateur detective novels of all time) and highly recommended by the dean of locked-room mystery scholars, Robert Adey, as "highly original." It's also one of the first popular novels to make use of Tibetan culture. Locked inside the Tibetan room of his Chicago apartment, the rich antiquarian was overheard repeating a forbidden occult chant under the watchful eyes of Buddhist gods. When the doors were opened, it appeared that he had succumbed to a heart attack. But the elderly Roman historian and sometime amateur sleuth Theocritus Lucius Westborough is convinced that Adam Merriweather's death was anything but natural and that the weapon was an eighth-century Tibetan manuscript.

Joan Coggin. *Who Killed the Curate?* Meet Lady Lupin Lorrimer Hastings, the young, lovely, scatterbrained and kindhearted newlywed wife to the vicar of St. Marks Parish in Glanville, Sussex. When it comes to matters clerical, she literally doesn't know Jews from Jesuits and she's hopelessly at sea at the meetings of the Mothers' Union, Girl Guides, or Temperance Society, but she's determined to make husband Andrew proud of her—or, at least, not to embarass him too badly. So when Andrew's curate is poisoned, Lady Lupin enlists the help of her old society pals, Duds and Tommy Lethbridge, as well as Andrew's nephew, a British secret service agent, to get at the truth. Lupin refuses to believe Diane Lloyd, the 38-year-old author of children's and detective stories, could have done the deed, and casts her net out over the other parishioners. All the suspects seem so nice, much more so than the victim, and Lupin announces she'll help the killer escape if only he or she confesses. Imagine Billie Burke, Gracie Allen or Pauline Collins of *No, Honestly* as a sleuth and you might get a tiny idea of what Lupin is like. Set at Christmas 1937 and first published in England in 1944, this is the first American appearance of *Who Killed the Curate?* "Coggin writes in the spirit of Nancy Mitford and E.M. Delafield. But the books are mysteries, so that makes them perfect."—Katherine Hall Page. "Marvelous."—*Deadly Pleasures* (0-915230-44-5, $14.00).

Manning Coles. The two English writers who collaborated as Coles are best known for those witty spy novels featuring Tommy Hambledon, but they also wrote four delightful—and funny—ghost novels. *The Far Traveller* (0-915230-35-6, 154 pages, $14.00) is a stand-alone novel in which a film company unknowingly hires the ghost of a long-dead German graf to play himself in a movie. "I laughed until I hurt. I liked it so much, I went back to page 1 and read it a second time."—Peggy Itzen, *Cozies, Capers & Crimes*. The other three books feature two cousins, one English, one American, and their spectral pet monkey who got a little drunk and tried to stop—futilely and fatally—a German advance outside a small French village during the 1870 Franco-Prussian War. Flash forward to the 1950s where this comic trio of friendly ghosts rematerialize to aid relatives in danger in *Brief Candles* (0-915230-24-0, 156 pages, $14.00), *Happy Returns* (0-915230-31-3, 156 pages, $14.00) and *Come and Go* (0-915230-34-8, 155 pages, $14.00).

Norbert Davis. There have been a lot of dogs in mystery fiction, from Baynard Kendrick's guide dog to Virginia Lanier's bloodhounds, but there's never been one quite like Carstairs. Doan, a short, chubby Los Angeles private eye, won Carstairs in a crap game, but there never is any question as to who the boss is in this relationship. Carstairs isn't just any Great Dane. He is so big that Doan figures he really ought to be considered another species. He scorns baby talk and belly rubs—unless administered by a pretty girl—and growls whenever Doan has a drink. His full name is Dougal's Laird Carstairs and as a sleuth he rarely barks up the wrong tree. In their first case, *The Mouse in the Mountain* (0-915230-41-0, 151 pages, $14.00), Carstairs is down in Mexico with Doan, ostensibly to convince a missing fugitive that he would do well to stay put. The case is complicated by three murders, assorted villains, and a horrific earthquake that cuts the mountainous little village of Los Altos off from the rest of Mexico. Doan and Carstairs aren't the only unusual visitors to Los Altos. There's Patricia Van Osdel, a ravishing blonde whose father made millions from flypaper, and Captain Emile Perona, a Mexican policeman whose long-ago Spanish ancestor helped establish Los Altos. It's that ancestor who brings teacher Janet Martin to Mexico along with a stolen book that may contain the key to a secret hidden for hundreds of years in the village church. Written in the snappy hardboiled style of the day, *The Mouse in the Mountain* was first published in 1943 and followed by two other Doan and Carstairs novels. "Each of these is fast-paced, occasionally lyrical in a hard-edged way, and often quite funny. Davis, in fact, was one of the few writers to successfully blend the so-called hardboiled story with farcical humor."—Bill Pronzini, *1001 Midnights.* Staff pick at The Sleuth of Baker Street in Toronto, Murder by the Book in Houston and The Poisoned Pen in Scotsdale. Four star review in *Romantic Times*. "A laugh a minute romp...hilarious dialogue and descriptions...utterly engaging, downright fun read...fetch this one! Highly recommended."—Michele A. Reed, *I Love a Mystery.* "Deft, charming...unique...one of my top ten all time favorite novels."—Ed Gorman, *Mystery Scene.* The second book, **Sally's in the Alley** (0-915230-46-1, $14.00), was equally well-received. *Publishers Weekly*: "Norbert Davis committed suicide in 1949, but his incomparable crime-fighting duo, Doan, the tippling private eye, and Carstairs, the huge and preternaturally clever Great Dane, march on in a re-release of the 1943 *Sally's in the Alley*, the second book in the dog-detective trilogy. Doan's on a government-sponsored mission to find an ore deposit in the Mojave Desert, but he's got to manage an odd (and oddly named) bunch of characters— Dust-Mouth Haggerty knows where the mine is but isn't telling; Doc Gravelmeyer's learning how undertaking can be a 'growth industry;' and film star Susan Sally's days are numbered—in an old-fashioned romp that matches its bloody crimes with belly laughs." The editor of *Mystery Scene* chimed in: "Enid and Tom Schantz, bless 'em, have just published the second novel by Norbert Davis, one of the most overlooked of all great pulp writers. This one is a comic look at the effects of WWII on the homefront. If you write fiction, or are thinking of writing fiction, or know someone who is writing fiction or is at least thinking of writing fiction, Davis is worth studying. John D. MacDonald always put him up, even admitted to imitating him upon occasion. I love Craig Rice. Davis is her equal."

Elizabeth Dean. Dean wrote only three mysteries, but in Emma Marsh she created one of the first independent female sleuths in the genre. Written in the screwball style of the 1930s, **Murder is a Collector's Item** (0-915230-19-4, $14.00) is described in a review in *Deadly Pleasures* by award-winning mystery writer Sujata Massey as a story that "froths over with the same effervescent humor as the best Hepburn-Grant films." Like the second book in the trilogy, **Murder is a Serious Business** (0-915230-

28-3, 254 pages, $14.95), it's set in a Boston antique store just as the Great Depression is drawing to a close. *Murder a Mile High* (0-915230-39-9, 188 pages, $14.00), moves to the Central City Opera House in the Colorado mountains, where Emma has been summoned by an old chum, the opera's reigning diva. Emma not only has to find a murderer, she may also have to catch a Nazi spy. A reviewer for a Central City area newspaper warmly greeted this reprint: "An endearing glimpse of Central City and Denver during World War II. . . . the dialogue twists and turns. . . . reads like a Nick and Nora movie. . . . charming."—*The Mountain-Ear.* "Fascinating."—*Romantic Times.*

Constance & Gwenyth Little. These two Australian-born sisters from New Jersey have developed almost a cult following among mystery readers. Critic Diane Plumley, writing in *Dastardly Deeds*, called their 21 mysteries "celluloid comedy written on paper." Each book, published between 1938 and 1953, was a stand-alone, but there was no mistaking a Little heroine. She hated housework, wasn't averse to a little gold-digging (so long as she called the shots), and couldn't help antagonizing cops and potential beaux. The Rue Morgue Press intends to reprint all of their books. Currently available: *The Black Coat* (0-915230-40-2, 155 pages, $14.00), *Black Corridors* (0-915230-33-X, 155 pages, $14.00), *The Black Gloves* (0-915230-20-8, 185 pages, $14.00), *Black-Headed Pins* (0-915230-25-9, 155 pages, $14.00), *The Black Honeymoon* (0-915230-21-6, 187 pages, $14.00), *The Black Paw* (0-915230-37-2, 156 pages, $14.00), *The Black Stocking* (0-915230-30-5, 154 pages, $14.00), *Great Black Kanba* (0-915230-22-4, 156 pages, $14.00), *The Grey Mist Murders* (0-915230-26-7, 153 pages, $14.00), and *The Black Eye* (0-915230-45-3, 154 pages, $14.00).

Marlys Millhiser. Our only non-vintage mystery, *The Mirror* (0-915230-15-1, 303 pages, $17.95) is our all-time bestselling book, now in a sixth printing. How could you not be intrigued by a novel in which "you find the main character marrying her own grandfather and giving birth to her own mother," as one reviewer put it of this supernatural, time-travel (sort-of) piece of wonderful make-believe set both in the mountains above Boulder, Colorado, at the turn of the century and in the city itself in 1978. Internet book services list scores of rave reviews from readers who often call it the "best book I've ever read."

James Norman. *Murder, Chop Chop* (0-915230-16-X, 189 pages,

$13.00) is a wonderful example of the eccentric detective novel. "The book has the butter-wouldn't-melt-in-his-mouth cool of Rick in *Casablanca*."—*The Rocky Mountain News*. "Amuses the reader no end."—*Mystery News*. "This long out-of-print masterpiece is intricately plotted, full of eccentric characters and very humorous indeed. Highly recommended."—*Mysteries by Mail*. Meet Gimiendo Hernandez Quinto, a gigantic Mexican who once rode with Pancho Villa and who now trains *guerrilleros* for the Nationalist Chinese government when he isn't solving murders. At his side is a beautiful Eurasian known as Mountain of Virtue, a woman as dangerous to men as she is irresistible. Together they look into the murder of Abe Harrow, an ambulance driver who appears to have died at three different times. First published in 1942.

Sheila Pim. *Ellery Queen's Mystery Magazine* said of these gentlel Irish village mysteries that Pim "depicts with style and humor everyday life." *Booklist* said they were in "the best tradition of Agatha Christie." ***Common or Garden Crime*** (0-915230-36-4, 157 pages, $14.00) is set in neutral Ireland during World War II when Lucy Bex must use her knowledge of gardening to keep the wrong person from going to the gallows. Beekeeper Edward Gildea uses his knowledge of bees and plants to do the same thing in ***A Hive of Suspects*** (0-915230-38-0, 155 pages, $14.00). ***Creeping Venom*** (0-915230-42-9, 155 pages, $14.00) mixes politics and religion into a deadly mixture.

Charlotte Murray Russell. Spinster sleuth Jane Amanda Edwards tangles with a murderer and Nazi spies in ***The Message of the Mute Dog*** (0-915230-43-7, 156 pages, $14.00), a culinary cozy set just before Pearl Harbor. Our earlier title, *Cook Up a Crime*, is currently out of print.

Juanita Sheridan. Sheridan was one of the most colorful figures in the history of detective fiction, as you can see from Tom and Enid Schantz's introduction to ***The Chinese Chop*** (0-915230-32-1, 155 pages, $14.00). Her books are equally colorful, as well as showing how mysteries with female protagonists began changing after World War II. The postwar housing crunch finds Janice Cameron, newly arrived in New York City from Hawaii, without a place to live until she answers an ad for a roommate. It turns out the advertiser is an acquaintance from Hawaii, Lily Wu, whom critic Anthony Boucher (for whom Bouchercon, the World Mystery Convention, is named) described as an "exquisitely blended product of Eastern and Western cultures" and the only female sleuth that he "was devotedly in love with," citing "that odd mixture of respect for her professional skills and delight in her personal charms." First published in 1949, this ground-breaking book was the first of four to feature Lily and be told by her Watson, Janice, a first-time novelist. No sooner do Lily and Janice move into a rooming house in Washington Square than a corpse is found in the basement. In Lily Wu, Sheridan created one of the most believable—and memorable—female sleuths of her day. "Highly recommended."—*I Love a Mystery*. "This well-written. . .enjoyable variant of the boarding house whodunit and a vivid portrait of the post WWII New York City housing shortage, puts to lie the common misconception that strong, self-reliant, non-spinster-or-comic sleuths didn't appear on the scene until the 1970s. Chinese-American Lily Wu and her novelist Watson, Janice Cameron, are young and feminine but not dependent on men."—*Ellery Queen's Mystery Magazine*. Look for more books in this series in 2002. Sheridan (who lived in Hawaii and left only weeks before the Japanese attack on Pearl Harbor in 1941) was a staunch advocate of the native Hawaiian people, as is shown in ***The Kahuna Killer***, 0-915230-47-X, $14.00 (first published in 1951). Critic Kathi Maio, writing in the August/September 1986 issue of *The Mystery Readers of America Journal*, praised the Lily Wu/Janice Cameron mystery series "for its non-polemical but very positive portrayals of women. Sheridan gives us many women in cameo and support roles. And their lives are as varied as the lives of men. They are doctors, dentists, agents, photographers, teachers, war heroes, and yes, femme fatales and earth mothers, too. It is, I think, no accident that some of the most positive portrayals in Sheridan's novels are of Asian and Pacific peoples…Sheridan is a refreshing relief from yellow menace thriller (and, for that matter, mysteries about benevolent Chinese patriarchs and daring Chinese masterminds. Sheridan obviously as no patience with racism. If a character speaks with contempt of Asian or Hawaiian culture, or refers to a Chinese as a 'gook' or a Hawaiian as a 'kanaka,' we know that that character is not a good guy. Often such characters meet with unhappy ends. Lily wastes little of her time berating whites for their racism. She shows the lie in who she is and how she lives her life." *The Kahuna Killer* marks Lily's and Janice's return to Hawaii where they find plenty of *pilikia*—trouble. Janice's dead father's files are stolen, her hostess is mysteriously ill, and a *kahuna* is seen performing the old rites in the native village on the beach. A childhood native friend warns that Janice that she is no longer welcome in his village. Ignoring his warnings, Janice sneaks down at night and discovers fresh blood on the ruined altar. Soon after, a sensuous native girl dances her last hula. Lily summons friends and relatives—her island irregulars—as she and Janice seek to stop the killer and save the little village.